SYSTEM OVERRIDE

THE AUTOMATED SERIES

BOOK 1

K. J. GILLENWATER

This is a work of fiction. Names, characters, places, and incidents are products of the author's imagination or are used fictitiously and are not to be construed as real. Any resemblance to actual events, locales, organizations, or persons, living or dead, is entirely coincidental.

System Override

ISBN Print: 979-8-9876112-6-5

ISBN eBook: 979-8-9876112-4-1

Cover by Miblart

CHAPTER 1
THE ANDROID

September 2043

I SAW my dead wife in Chicago today.

Her face stood out among hundreds of other faces, impossible to miss: the curve of her jaw, the tipped up nose, the eyes a bit too close together, and the red hair. Long, wavy, thick. A billowing fan of red as she walked in the opposite direction. The notorious Chicago wind tumbled through it in a forceful gust, and she swept the strands out of her eyes and continued past me.

Without a look. Without an acknowledgment.

The wind had caught her hair in the same way it used to when we worked the ranch together, whipping it across her face in unruly waves. A familiar ache bloomed, as if my body remembered the loss before my mind did.

It was as if I saw a ghost in broad daylight.

Five years of marriage flashed by in seconds.

Impossible.

I spun for a second look, colliding with a businessman whose transparent tablet display flickered on impact. He muttered a curse, but I barely registered it. In a city built on constant motion, I was the disruption, the stone in the stream.

That's when I realized her hair was too red, too perfect. The sway of her hips was eerily symmetrical, unnervingly precise. Someone had created a near-exact android replica of my wife.

I closed my hand around the marble I carried in my pocket —a shooter made of sparkling glass. A beauty. My lucky charm. I rolled my thumb cross its smooth, cool surface as I followed the lookalike down the street.

My presentation at the Drake Hotel loomed in less than an hour, six months of preparation for the 2043 Farming and Ranching Symposium gone to waste. But I didn't care. All that mattered was finding out why she existed—this machine version of Meredith.

I forced my way through the crowds and followed her around the corner, heading away from Lake Michigan. A group of teenagers swarmed the sidewalk, laughing and shoving one another as the bracelets they wore projected different holographic images. I weaved through them, never taking my eyes off the back of her head. I was closing the gap, and yet the fear she'd vanish into the chaos at any second kept me moving more quickly.

What madness was this? Androids were strictly regulated. But even the androids I'd seen back home had never looked this good, this real, this *human*. No one else on the crowded street would recognize this attractive woman as an imposter. Only someone who knew her. Who loved her.

A dull thud in my chest reminded me of the sorrow I'd tried to bury. The memories of her returned in a mental assault. For a split second I wondered, what if I could touch her? The android. The fake woman a half-a-block in front of me. What if I could meet her, talk to her? Would she have the same voice? The same smile with the twisted canine tooth?

I wanted to believe she would be the same.

She crossed the busy street, dodging a few honking cars. I approached the curb to do the same, but a firm hand on my arm stopped me.

"Eli, hey, I thought that was you," said John Tellman, a neighboring rancher who liked all the newfangled gadgets and farming methods they displayed at the Symposium. His broad face beamed. "Can't believe you actually made it this year. I thought you hated these things."

I watched as she disappeared into a mirrored skyscraper with CALLAHAN, INC. emblazoned above its entrance.

I'd heard whispers about Callahan, Inc.—rumors of clandestine projects, legal battles with the government, and corporate rivalries. But this? This was different. This was personal.

"Eli?"

I blinked. She was gone, swallowed by the massive building. But curiosity burned inside me. Why create such a perfect replica? What purpose did she serve? Who made her? It was not cheap to build such a thing. Especially one that was so realistic.

"I agreed to give a talk," I finally answered. Thirty minutes ago, my head had been full of the presentation I'd prepared: *Traditional Sheep Ranching in the Modern Era.* Now my mind was full of memories of my wife, our life together on the ranch, and her yearly trip to the Midwest. Alone. Without me. I'd never questioned it. Never once. I'd loved her. She had a past. It didn't bother me.

But maybe I should have. The android couldn't be a coincidence.

"Are you okay?" John asked.

"Why do you ask?"

"You're shaking."

I looked down at my fisted hands. He was right. A tenseness had gripped my body. "I'm fine," I lied, forcing myself to relax. "Have you registered yet?"

He nodded. "Last night."

As I stepped away from the curb, the pedestrian traffic grew heavier. We were blocking the flow.

"Want to help me set up?" I needed the distraction.

As we made our way toward the hotel, I clung to a single thought: I saw my dead wife, Meredith, downtown today.

CHAPTER 2
AN INVITATION

THE HALL where my speech was scheduled to be presented was much larger than I anticipated. My armpits grew damp. But I headed straight for the steps that led to the stage and hoped John wouldn't notice my anxiety. Perhaps once I had everything set up, my nerves would settle. I wasn't accustomed to being stared at. My natural habitat was my two thousand acres of ranch land and my closest friends were my dog, Spark, and the fifteen hundred sheep I raised.

"Mr. Zurbano," a tall, lithe blonde woman had followed us on stage and stretched a hand out to me. "So glad to finally meet you." Confusion must've been clear on my face, because she added, "I'm Samantha Callahan, one of the main sponsors for the symposium this year."

I shook her hand. A cloud of her lavender-scented perfume filled my nose. "Callahan?" I thought about the building into which the android copy of my wife had disappeared moments before my neighbor had recognized me. The hair rose on the back of my neck.

"Callahan makes some of the best herding drones on the market," John explained as he set a pitcher of water on the podium, as if I didn't know the name 'Callahan.' He seemed to relish the role of helper. Not many sheep ranchers from Idaho were invited to speak at such a prestigious conference. I'd be the talk of Kemper Creek when I returned home.

Was it only coincidence that the lookalike Meredith had chosen their headquarters as her destination?

"Right. However, I'm not sure why you'd have any interest in my presentation, Ms. Callahan." Although her name sparked my curiosity, I masked my reaction. I'd have time later to dig into her background and see if I could find any link she might have to my wife. "I'm a huge proponent of less modern methods of ranching. The outcomes are better. When you're merely keeping an eye on your animals from a camera in the sky, you don't have the same connection to them."

"That's a bit of an outdated view." Samantha smiled, but her eyes sharpened. "I'll admit your presentation might attract a crowd for nostalgia reasons—romanticizing how our grandfathers and great-grandfathers used to ranch—but I don't understand what it has to do with the symposium. You're presenting obsolete traditional ways, while I'm here to promote our most important new advancements."

"The event organizers approached me about participating. They must believe I have something of value to add to the discussion," I said as I flipped through my transparent smart cards, each one displaying my notes in digital text.

My neighbor joined me in the middle of the stage. "I'm all for innovative approaches, but if older strategies provide better outcomes, why aren't we allowed to discuss them? I thought this event was open to any and all innovators," John said. "There's nothing wrong with incorporating a little of the old with the new."

"I certainly hope not," said a deep voice from the footlights. "We want to be the most technologically advanced conference in the world, but still provide topics of interest to our attendees."

A man in a navy suit stepped onto the stage, his salt and pepper hair tipping me off that he was older than me by at least ten years.

"Mr. Zurbano, I wanted to stop by before your speech to make sure everything was going smoothly. I'm the one who asked for you to submit a presentation."

I scoured my brain for a name. "Joe Cross?"

"Yes, a pleasure to meet you in person."

We shook hands.

"I don't think you've ever made it to our symposiums in the past," Joe continued, "but your traditional approach sure was a hot topic at last year's event. They said you were the only ranch that avoided the Bluetongue outbreak in the West."

I shrugged. "I'm pretty independent when it comes to my methods."

Back home, most ranchers followed government guidelines for ranching and herd health. Something about having dictates from Washington D.C.—thousands of miles from ranch lands and the people who worked them—rubbed me the wrong way. Perhaps it was my Basque background. My family's history traced back to the shepherds of the Pyrenees, a group which valued independence, tradition, and the land itself. We were a different breed. I'd been raised to stick close to my roots and methods that had proven successful for our family for hundreds of years.

The older man gave a nod of recognition to Ms. Callahan. "Samantha, I'm surprised to see you here. I wouldn't think this topic would interest you."

"I saw the name Zurbano on the list of speakers. I've heard things. Call me curious." Her pale skin stretched taut over her cheeks and chin, and her teeth appeared too straight to be real.

"Besides, I've had a longing to visit Idaho. Someone I once knew told me it was a beautiful place." Her blue gaze connected with mine.

A ripple of dread ran through me.

* * *

After wrapping up my presentation, I offered polite smiles and brief handshakes to the lingering crowd of ranchers who wanted to chat about heritage-based techniques. Normally, I would have welcomed the conversation, but I needed space to think. Not that long ago, I had been looking forward to sharing my knowledge with others, but after the encounter with the lookalike of my wife on the streets of the city, my adrenaline was still surging.

Ms. Callahan had vanished after my talk. I'd searched for her in the crowd, but couldn't find the tall, slim figure with the platinum blonde hair anywhere.

I gave my excuses to John, turning down his invitation for a drink at the bar. I'd only be in town for a week, and I wasn't going to waste it on symposium socials or idle chatter. Every waking minute would be spent searching for answers.

As I headed up to my room, the hallway was quiet except for the soft hum of an android maid pushing a cart. It was one of the regular ones. Not the hyper-realistic version I'd seen earlier. Her joints were stiff, her movements jerky, her features plastic and devoid of expression. The same type I'd noticed in Kemper Creek sweeping sidewalks in summer and scooping snow in winter. A few big ranchers with deep pockets used them for the more mundane physical chores.

I slowed my steps, my thoughts revisiting the encounter on the street. The idea that someone had created an android

Meredith replica so advanced, so unlike any other I'd ever seen, turned my world upside down.

The maid reacted to my presence. "Sir, would you like turndown service? In which room are you staying?"

Its empty eyes looked at me.

"No, thank you."

"As you wish, sir," the maid said in its mechanical, expressionless voice.

I passed her by and reached my room—541. As I touched my hand to the door handle, it instantly unlocked. Handprint activated. The desk clerk had scanned my palm in the lobby when I'd checked in.

I spied a small red card on the floor.

I picked it up, shut the door, and flipped it over. The blank card lit up, and I detected a familiar lavender scent. A cool piece of tech I hadn't experienced before. Letters appeared, forming a message:

> Mr. Zurbano,
> Please join me for dinner downstairs. Seven o'clock sharp.
> Samantha Callahan

The words glowed brighter and brighter until they were almost blinding. The whole card turned into a blast of white light. Then it crumpled into itself and disappeared into nothing but a wisp of lavender-scented smoke.

Ms. Callahan sure liked to make an impression. But she'd implied I wasn't that interesting. She thought my presentation topic boring and outdated. What possible reason did she have to dine with me? Was I an anachronism? Maybe she was going to show me off to her rich friends. A silly sheep rancher from podunk Idaho who believed animals were better company than high-powered folks from the city.

But her words earlier had intrigued me. She claimed to recognize my name. I didn't believe her, but why had she said that? Her connection to Callahan, Inc. made my nerves jump. The rumors I'd heard about the company—dark whispers of unethical experiments, advanced projects buried beneath layers of corporate secrecy. Finding out everything about her company, her family, and that towering building might reveal why a Meredith robot was walking the streets. The possibilities sickened me.

After the symposium ended on Wednesday, I'd intended to take a little time to explore the city. But now I focused only on my wife. The crude replica—for that's what it was in my mind —made me angry. Meredith had loved me, and I had loved her. I aimed to honor her memory. Allowing an android to exist who looked like her twin gave me an eerie sense of dread.

When I crossed the threshold into the bathroom, the lights switched on automatically. I asked the faucet for ninety-two degree water. A waterfall poured out. I splashed some on my face. I could do this. I could have dinner with Samantha Callahan and, if I kept my emotions in check, find out what she knew about advanced androids who were indistinguishable from humans.

I grabbed a towel, dried my face, and mentally prepared for the date.

Back on the ranch, my sheep responded best to a firm hand. I couldn't back down, even when doing difficult work. The only way to maintain the health of the flock sometimes involved treating disease, trimming hooves, helping birth the lambs in spring.

My wife had commented on my ability to set aside my emotions when working these tasks. Tonight, I would draw on the talent I had developed since my youth. I'd shut down my feelings and do the work necessary to track down the people responsible for building a robot that shouldn't exist. And then I'd make them sorry they'd ever done it.

* * *

The sumptuous dining room of the Palm Court restaurant in the Drake Hotel hadn't changed in decades. Its classic all white decor appealed to the royalty and wealthy who'd dined here, looking for an atmosphere far removed from the chaos outside on the busy streets. The restaurant exuded early 1900s beauty and refinement, whereas East Walton Place reflected how much Chicago had changed in the one-hundred and twenty years since the Drake's opening. From the days of the massive Union Stock Yards—four hundred and fifty acres with animal pens, railroad chutes, and office buildings—to a modern city of steam-cleaned sidewalks and polished marble facades. Quite a shift. And most of it made possible with the help of androids who worked through the night to ensure the dirt and grime of the day was scrubbed clean by morning.

I'd brought one suit with me—the one I had been married in. I tugged at the sleeves. It was a far cry from my usual attire of blue jeans and wool shirt.

"Well, don't you clean up nicely?" A waft of lavender scent accompanied the voice.

I turned to see Samantha Callahan arrive in a figure hugging gold gown that brought out the highlights in her hair. She was an attractive woman, and she knew it.

"I suppose." I'd made my way downstairs rather confidently. With the extra hour I had, I'd done my best to research Callahan, Inc. and its Chief Executive Officer, Samantha Callahan. She was a tech prodigy, known for her groundbreaking work in robotics before taking over the family business when her father retired. A coincidence that stood out. "Nice to see you again, Ms. Callahan." I offered up my hand.

She ignored it. "I'm glad you accepted my invitation."

I recalled the neat little note paper with the glowing letters that had disappeared. "That was an impressive bit of technology."

Her face remained expressionless—the very definition of an ice queen. "This dinner is just between you and me. Nobody else needs to know we met."

A secret meeting with a vanishing invite? Interesting.

"I hope you'll excuse me if I don't know how to behave." I gestured at the opulence surrounding us as the tuxedoed maitre d' approached. "I'm from the country, and I'm not quite used to such surroundings." I gave a tight smile.

"Don't be so coy, Mr. Zurbano. You're not a stupid man." She gave the maitre d' a brief, curt nod as he led us to a table near a grand curtained column that had a beige-padded bench on one side and a cream chair on the other.

Ms. Callahan slid gracefully onto the bench. I took the chair opposite.

After the maitre d' handed us our menus, I posed the question I'd been waiting to ask, "Why am I here?"

She peered at me over the top of her menu. "I was fascinated by your remarks and wanted to hear more about your ranch in Idaho. Our company is always looking to expand into new markets."

She was lying. What she said didn't match the expression in her eyes—cold, detached. I'd bored her. "You left before I'd finished." I unbuttoned by jacket. The warmth in the room suddenly overpowering.

My mind leapt to my beautiful Meredith and the last time I'd seen her alive—her skin pallid, her features sunken into her face, her body wasted away. Then I was reminded of the mechanical caricature of her. Too perfect, too bright, too everything. Samantha Callahan knew something, and that is why she brought me here.

Her lips curved up in an unfeeling smile. "Did I? I hope you didn't think I was rude."

Our server approached with a carafe of water and began to pour. "Who told you about me?" The ice clinked in the goblets, emphasizing my words.

Ms. Callahan was unhurried. She closed her menu, set it to one side, picked up her glass, and took a sip of water before saying, "Why, Eli, your wife, of course."

CHAPTER 3
MEREDITH'S SECRETS

MY MIND BLANKED. I didn't know how to respond. This made no sense. Meredith knew Samantha Callahan, the CEO of the third largest company in Chicago? A wealthy woman who was born into one of the Windy City's most storied families, who was educated at Northwestern, who now was worth billions of dollars and on track to be worth billions more if their latest agricultural drones operated as well as promised?

"Ah," she said with a crocodile smile, "you didn't know." She set down her water glass, rested her elbows on the table, and tented her hands. "I thought this might be an interesting dinner. Much more interesting than what I had planned for tonight—a cocktail party with Joe Cross and the rest of the symposium board. They're desperate to lockdown our sponsorship for next year's conference. I was the one who suggested you as a speaker, by the way. I hoped it would add a touch of authenticity to the event." Her eyes lingered on me, as if she were gauging my reaction.

I accidentally spilled some water. It created a dark stain on the tablecloth, evidence of my shock. Samantha had a hand in inviting me here?

Since we'd both put down our menus, the server approached. "Madame, are you ready to order?"

Her attention swung away from me for a few seconds. "We'd like the Filet Mignon and Shrimp En Croute." She looked across the table at me. "That is, unless you are allergic to shellfish?"

I shook my head. This woman was used to being in charge. Knowing she'd brought me here, I had to tread carefully. If I played along, would she be more likely to give me answers?

"Wonderful." She handed her menu to the server. "We'll also have that Cabernet Sauvignon I had the last time I was here. The Napa Valley one. So fantastic." With a quick up-tilt of her lips, she made it seem as if we were two friends sharing a meal.

"Very good, madame." He clicked his heels and headed to the kitchen.

"Pretty realistic, isn't he?" My dinner date kept her gaze on the man.

"The waiter?" I still hadn't formulated the questions I wanted to ask about Meredith. That very first year we were married came back to me. The strange request she'd had. The one I'd granted without hesitation.

"Yes, he's one of ours." With a flourish, she shook out her white cloth napkin and laid it across her lap. "Our family is close friends with the owner of the Drake. We've been developing more realistic androids, and Charles offered to try them out. It's been a fruitful experiment so far." She gestured at the rest of the diners in the restaurant. "I don't imagine any of them realize they're being served by an android. Do you think they'll leave a good tip?" She laughed.

So now I knew for certain that Callahan, Inc. was doing more than creating agricultural machinery. "How did you know my wife?" Did I want the answer? Who was Meredith before she appeared in Kemper Creek six years ago with a single suitcase and driving a thirty-year-old pickup truck that still ran on gasoline?

Ms. Callahan's dress shimmered under the soft lighting. "We were dear old friends. I feel as if I've known her my whole life." Her forehead wrinkled. "I'm sorry to hear she passed away."

Her words cut deeper than I expected. Somehow, hearing sympathies from a rich woman who was a complete stranger to me yet knew my wife intimately grated against something raw inside of me. The urge overcame me to push back from the table and walk out. This socialite with her fancy dress and refined manners set my teeth on edge. All the hours I put in to keep my ranch afloat out on the ATV, putting up hay, caring for my animals in the cold, the wet, and the heat—this woman had no idea what life really was. What living really was. She relied on androids and servants to make her life one of ease. She spent her billions on private jets and mansions and things I'd never even dream of doing.

But I couldn't leave. I'd allowed Meredith to have her secrets because I loved her. I told her I didn't need to know all the details. I could still be the husband she needed without understanding the reason for her actions.

But now that she was gone? Now that she would never come back? I couldn't stand the idea of those secrets existing and people like Samantha knowing them.

If I couldn't have my wife back, I sure as hell was going to find out everything about her. Every goddamn thing.

"You've grown so quiet," said my attractive dining companion. "I'm sorry if I upset you."

Before I could answer, the sommelier reached our table with a bottle of wine. I found myself eyeballing his movements. Was he an android, too?

Samantha smoothly pushed her goblet closer to the edge of the table. "Wine makes everything better, doesn't it?" Her voice was as smooth as silk, and a lock of her shiny blonde hair slipped onto her exposed shoulder.

I couldn't remember when I'd last had a glass of wine. Maybe at an anniversary dinner with my wife at the nicest restaurant in Kemper Creek—there were only three worth visiting for a special occasion. But more than likely, we'd only had a choice between red wine or white. "I don't drink much."

The sommelier had a balding head, a mustache that twitched as he waited for Ms. Callahan to taste the vintage, and a bead of sweat gathering at his temple.

Human. Most definitely human. Had to be.

When the man had poured our two glasses and left the bottle on the table, Samantha finished her first full sip and said, "Did you wonder if he was one, too?"

"Hmm?" I swirled the red wine in my glass and admired its rich ruby color under the muted lighting. If I had to sit through a fancy meal with a stranger to learn more about my own wife, I might as well enjoy it. I took a sip. The robust notes of black-berry and mint hit my tongue.

"Nice, isn't it?" She seemed to take delight in my enjoy-ment of the wine she'd chosen—as if I were a child to be spoiled.

I nodded and set down my glass. "He isn't."

"Isn't what?"

"A robot."

Her eyes lit up. "Ah, you are observant, aren't you?" She raised her head slightly to seek out the sommelier. "What did you observe? We're always looking for ways to make our new product more believable."

"He was nervous, sweating." Should I have revealed the hint that helped me determine his humanity?

"Was he?" She lifted her hand limply into the air and tapped a finger on her full bottom lip. "I'll have to jot that down and send a memo to our engineering team."

Enough of this boring dialogue. I should use the meeting to my advantage. Who knew if I'd ever have the opportunity to question her one on one again? "When did Callahan, Inc. decide to enter the android market? I thought your company was mainly an agricultural firm—the herding drones, solar-powered autonomous tractors, automated herbicide sprayers—"

"We only recommend natural weed deterrents, just to clarify."

I ignored her attempt at starting up an environmental debate. With food costs climbing, I'd prefer to have the best methods survive for more robust harvests, but that would have to wait for another day. Possibly my next symposium topic. "But androids? Human-looking androids. Why would Callahan be interested?"

Her pretty face froze, as if she'd had one too many injections of the latest wrinkle eraser. "It's smart business. Androids are the future of the world. Imagine if you could relax on your ranch and let machines do the work. Menial tasks aren't worth your time, are they?"

"We have androids like that already." I pointed at the ceiling. "The maid who cleans my room? Android. The luggage handlers at the airport? Android. Probably the janitor in your fancy Callahan headquarters, too. Why would you need to fool people into believing they're real humans?" I couldn't help but think of robot Meredith. How upsetting it had been to see her walking the streets of the city.

She blanched.

Had I exposed something more sinister under the surface at her family business?

My cell phone buzzed in my pocket. I unrolled it. A text from John Tellman.

> Someone's in your room. Where are you?

My gaze met hers. Had I been lured here so someone had an opportunity to search my room?

I pushed back my chair. "Unfortunately, I have to go. Thank you for the invitation, and I'm sorry I'll miss dinner. The wine, however, was delightful." I took another sip before stepping away from the table.

"Wait." Samantha held up her hand. "Your steak."

But her face crumbled as it dawned on her the ruse had been exposed. She knew that I knew.

Why would she want someone to look through my things?

***

"I'm glad we had rooms on the same floor." John Tellman met me at the elevators. "Or who knows what would've happened?"

By the time I arrived, I'd removed my jacket and rolled up the sleeves of my white dress shirt. "Did you find out who was in my room?"

"No, but it wasn't the maid. That's for sure." My friend wore the same clothes he'd had on at the symposium earlier. He must've found someone else interested in taking him up on the offer of sharing a drink. "I saw him leave. Tall, dark hair, all in black."

"Did you call the police?" I slipped my hand into my pants pocket and rubbed my thumb across my marble. It soothed me and made me feel as if I were back home looking out the kitchen window at the southern pasture.

"No, but I did contact the front desk. They're sending up their security team."

That wouldn't do. Not at all. "Call them back." I was in a game of cat and mouse with Samantha and her family's business. I didn't trust the police to be on my side in a place that relied on Callahan, Inc. for a substantial amount of revenue. "Tell them everything's fine."

"But your room. Someone broke in." He held his phone tightly. "Who knows what they stole? Don't you want to make sure that nothing's missing first?" John rubbed a calloused hand over his neck. "Besides, management should be warned that a thief was roaming the halls. This is a five-star hotel. They have a reputation to uphold. At the very least, they should offer you some kind of compensation. Aren't these new door locking systems supposed to be secure?"

I reflected on the palm scan I'd received in the lobby when I checked in the night before. "The maid can enter my room." Was it merely an artificial security measure to make guests feel safer?

"Only if you set the door to 'Maid Service.'"

I struggled to remember if I'd pushed the button to indicate I wanted the maid. The invitation to dinner had distracted me. I'd been so eager to learn why Samantha wanted to see me. I had to be more careful next time. "And how does she get in?"

The maid I'd seen earlier. Had the robot given someone access? Who programmed and maintained the robot staff? Then I reflected on Samantha's words, and the relationship she had with the hotel owner.

I started down the hallway to my room. John scrambled to keep up with me. "Are you sure you want me to cancel security?"

"Yes." I was taller than John by a few inches, and I heard

him breathing hard behind me in his attempts to match my pace.

He made the call.

My door stood ajar. A shiver crept up my back. The Maid Service light glowed next to the elaborate brass door knob. Gently, I pushed it open. The contents of my suitcase had been dumped on the bed, and my attaché, where I'd stored the smart cards and materials for my presentation, had been spilled on the floor.

"Damn." John had caught up to me. "Who would do this? Before I was able to move, he headed for the bed. "Can you tell if anything's missing?"

"I don't know." I scooped up the papers and smart cards and shoved them back inside the attaché. "I didn't bring much with me and certainly nothing valuable."

Although there was no evidence of it, it was obvious this had been Samantha Callahan's doing. Her expression at the dinner table when I excused myself said it all. But why? Did this have something to do with the android replica of my wife? No one even realized I'd seen her.

John picked up a pair of pants that had slipped from the bed to the floor. "I still think you should let the hotel know about this."

I pawed through the clothes. "Looks as if everything is here."

"Meredith would've agreed with me." My neighbor handed me my socks. "You can't handle it all by yourself, Eli. Did you know she told me to keep an eye on you? She worried about what might happen after she was gone."

"Shut up," I said sharply. My mind was a swirl of emotions: confusion, anger, sorrow. "Don't speak her name again."

John leaned away from me. "I'm sorry," he said quietly. "I didn't mean to offend you. That woman loved you, Eli. Loved you with everything she had." He headed toward the door. "Some men dream of a wife like that." Before I had a chance to react, he slipped out into the hall.

I closed my eyes and remembered Meredith before she grew ill—smiling as she leaned against the old fence, the sun catching her red hair. I almost heard her laugh, teasing me for letting the sheep wander too close to her failing vegetable patch. Before she came into my life, I never realized how much I was missing. Now, the emptiness left behind was hard to ignore.

I sat on the bed, with my clothes strewn about me, and longed to have her back.

CHAPTER 4
TOUR APPROVED

THE DAY MEREDITH PAUL arrived in Kemper Creek had been a day worth remembering. We'd had an early snowstorm —mid-October—and any road except the main highway had been undrivable. The snow had been wet and deep—a bad combination that would turn into ice before the robot plows cleared the back roads. And my ranch happened to sit on one of them, a gravel road that ran between Highway 15 and Leadore. The locals called it Railroad Canyon, and it wended its way up into the mountains and back down again through some of the prettiest country in the West.

Guess Meredith had thought it was pretty, too, when she'd turned off the highway and attempted to drive it—until she got stuck, that is.

I saw her from my kitchen window. The old pickup kicked up snow as she dug herself in even deeper. When I strolled out to the barn to start up my grandfather's vintage tractor to give a stranger a hand, I had no idea how my life would change.

I'd hooked up a chain to the rusty bumper of her Ford, hauled her out of the mire she'd gotten herself into, and invited her back inside for some coffee. It would be some time before the roads would be cleared enough for traffic. Besides, I liked her name.

Meredith Paul.

Could you fall in love with someone merely because of her name? It was an old-fashioned one that was a throwback to simpler times. Whoever had given it to this woman must have had a respect or a love of the traditional. Meredith. It traveled through my mind in a pleasant way, reminding me of picnics on the shore of the Salmon River in August, when everything was dry as a bone, but the days were long and warm and lovely.

As we sat at the kitchen table, watching the clock tick and the snow continue to fall, I'd hoped the storm would never end. I wanted to carry on just like this: quiet talking, shy smiles.

I'd handed her a fresh cup of coffee, and when she'd touched my arm, it seared me like a brand.

* * *

I lay on my bed in my hotel room, wide awake. After the strange meal with Samantha Callahan and the break-in, sleep escaped me. John had left over an hour ago with a reminder that I should speak with the general manager in the morning about it. I'd agreed, but my thoughts drifted elsewhere.

I had to find her again—the android, who looked like my wife. I must know more. The sight of her face brought back our years together in sharp color. Memories leaped into my head as if everything happened yesterday: our meeting, falling in love, getting married, hoping for a family, and then her unexpected illness.

As the clock moved past midnight, I devised a plan. I didn't have much time to work with, so each day mattered. The mystery of Samantha's interest in me and the contents of my room made me wonder if someone had seen the encounter with my wife's robot twin. Or was I being paranoid? It had been less than a minute. A flash of red hair, the curve of a cheek, and then she'd disappeared.

I grabbed my tablet and unfolded it. Then I tapped on the screen and navigated to the Callahan website. They offered industrial tours with advance notice. Looked as if it was more about their drone assembly line and engineering department than a tour of the whole building. But it would get me in the door. I filled out an interest form, informed them of the shortened schedule I was dealing with and my connection to the symposium, and hoped for the best.

Restless, I climbed off the bed and headed for the window that looked out over Chicago's streets. Massive video screens decorated the night, advertising restaurants, products, hotels, and more. My gaze went beyond the garish images and scanned the building silhouettes. Finally, I recognized the mirrored facade of Callahan, Inc.—a sleek tower that seemed to absorb the city around it. The surface reflected the neon lights and passing shadows. It loomed quietly, a modern monolith.

"Tomorrow," I said and placed my hand against the glass.

To keep my neighbor, John Tellman, from worrying and asking too many questions, I made sure to attend the Symposium's Breakfast with the Keynote Speaker the next morning, a world-renowned expert in Agricultural Economics from the University of Chicago. His name eluded me, but I knew he'd drawn an audience at the casual bar gathering after the first day of presentations. This morning was the same, as a group of attendees huddled around a medium-size man with graying curly hair. Their gazes were fixed, as if each word was a data stream they didn't want to miss. Acolytes of his theories on the economics of modern ranching.

As I carried my plate of ethically sourced scrambled eggs and locally made cheeses past the growing crowd, my phone vibrated in my pocket. I chose a table in the furthest corner against a wall, hoping no one would join me.

Callahan's PR department had responded to my tour request. Eagerly, I read the reply.

Tour approved. Please meet your guide in the Callahan Building lobby at nine a.m. sharp. No photography allowed. Security scans will be required. Dress accordingly.

My heart skipped a few beats. Nerves tingled. I asked for this. I wanted a chance to see inside the building, find out if the Fake Meredith appeared, ask if someone knew her. I was playing it by ear, which wasn't my style. I preferred to be planned. My life adhered to a distinct schedule: up by six, breakfast by six thirty, chores in the barn by seven—pulling the hay, filling the water basin, then checking in on the lambs and their mothers, and on and on. Every day was much the same, and that's how I liked it. I knew when the seasons changed and the work followed the seasons. Winter, spring, summer, fall. Over and over, with reassuring regularity. As my Basque ancestors did decades before me.

But the idea to ask for a tour stemmed mostly from emotion. It gnawed at me. Mistakes were made when one relied on feelings to make decisions. I took a bite of my eggs, and they tasted like ash on my tongue. I only had thirty minutes to really decide if I was going to follow through on my plan.

I re-read the message: "Security scans will be required."

Was that due to corporate espionage? Were there truly

security concerns at an agricultural equipment company? Or was it their 'secret' hyper realistic androids? Perhaps Samantha had revealed a little too much about what they were up to last night.

As I was taking my final swig of coffee, Tellman emerged from the crowd by the Keynote Speaker. If I waited much longer, he'd notice me, and I didn't want to be noticed or he might get in the way of my plans. John, with his practical mindset and well-meaning idea of being my minder while in Chicago, meant I had to escape before he saw me.

I slipped from my chair, leaving my half-empty plate and mug on the table. Out in the hall, I re-buttoned a cuff and wondered if my clothing would be appropriate for the tour—dress slacks and a button-down shirt with no tie.

When I reached the sidewalk, a puff of steam erupted from a nearby grate, spitting out a sulfurous stench that lingered in the heavy air. On the streets, air cars wove through the traffic, their sleek forms quietly braking then accelerating to take advantage of any minute gap between vehicles. Worker robots shuffled by, their movements jerky, sweeping debris into neat piles or walking someone's beloved Dachshund or miniature Poodle.

The city was a restless, humming machine, full of life but somehow devoid of soul. I missed the clean, fresh air of my ranch in Idaho, where the scent of sagebrush mixed with the earthy notes of wet soil and new grass. Meredith called it a magic place that made her feel calm and whole.

Seeing the place she'd come from, I understood what she meant.

I strode in the direction of the Callahan headquarters. It wasn't much of a walk. At the corner, I waited for the light with a host of Chicagoans headed to work or school. Some wore backpacks and shorts, others carried briefcases and had donned suits. I'd never seen so many cars and pedestrians in one place at one time. For a moment, I felt claustrophobic. Not so much from the people, but from the noise. Taxis honked, buses rumbled—a cacophony echoed in the canyon of buildings.

I focused on my destination. At the next corner, I would make a right.

Would I see her again? Or was Robot Meredith only a figment of my imagination?

The glare of the morning sun bounced off the building's mirrored exterior. I paused, observing a few people pass through the steel-framed entrance. They moved with robotic efficiency, faces impassive, their footsteps quick and methodical. It was as if the building itself demanded their obedience—an imposing edifice that swallowed them without acknowledgment, like a machine taking in parts.

An empty feeling hit the pit of my stomach. The doors, automated and smooth, slid open without a sound. I stepped inside, the interior air cooler, sterile, and stripped of any welcome.

CHAPTER 5
SECURITY SCAN

THE INTERIOR of the Callahan building was the equivalent of walking into Carlsbad Caverns. Despite the glistening exterior with its dozens of mirrored windows, the lobby was dark. The windows, at least the ones covering the lobby outside, weren't real. They were fake. The walls were painted a deep blue and rose thirty feet into the air. Complicated chandeliers with twists and turns and tiny little bulbs hung high above, looking like stars in the night sky. Antique lamps and overstuffed armchairs created dim, cozy spaces around the edges while in the center stood a well-lit desk with two identically dressed people behind it. One man, one woman. Both wore navy blue slacks that matched the walls and stiff white shirts with tall collars that brushed the lobes of their ears.

Although the gigantic lobby exuded the feeling of being inside a cave, a pleasant cinnamon odor filled the space. I took a quick glance around with some strange hope I'd see Fake Meredith sitting in one of the chairs, maybe reading a printed book like my wife used to do. But the room was empty of people except for me and the two manning the desk.

"May I help you, sir?" the woman asked.

As I approached her, I realized she was an android. Not

like the waiter last night, but the usual type—pale face with a metallic undertone, a voice without much inflection, and the dead eyes. Eyes that stared, but didn't see. It was hard to describe how I perceived these robots, but it was why I avoided them when possible back home. The eyes. So empty. So devoid of anything.

I unrolled my phone to show her the message I'd received. "I'm here for the tour?"

The robot woman, with a name tag that read Ann, scanned my phone screen. Her mechanical body froze. Jerkily, she turned her head toward her companion. "Do we have a tour scheduled for this morning, Bob?"

Bob the Robot levitated his hand over the desk behind the counter. The screen embedded in it came to life. His finger flicked, and the display scrolled through a document he'd pulled up. "No, Ann, we do not have a tour scheduled this morning." He looked up and stared at me blankly.

The awkward back and forth was maddening. These robot receptionists were programmed to pretend to be human, but they'd been given annoying verbiage to recite that only slowed things down. "It's 8:55 a.m." I showed them the time on my phone. "My tour starts at 9 a.m. sharp. Where do the tours begin?"

Who cared what the robots believed to be true on their stupid schedule? If they could only think logically like a real person, they would be able to follow some sort of mental decision tree. But, instead, their 'thinking' ended at the screen in front of them.

"We do not have a tour scheduled this morning," Ann the Robot repeated Bob word for word.

My eyelids flickered. If I had to, I would find a human being somewhere to ask. I only had a matter of days to hunt for the lookalike robot, my wife's mechanical twin, and I wasn't going to let programmed idiots block my way.

Near the desk in a far corner, I spied a door. Perhaps this would be where I'd find an elevator, an office, something that would be staffed by real humans.

Ignoring the protests of the two robot receptionists, I strode past them and headed straight for it.

"Sir, you must not enter," Ann the Robot protested. "Sir, you must not enter."

Her manufactured feet, in precise rhythm, followed me on the marble floor. Clack. Clack. Clack.

I reached the door and grasped the doorknob.

A dark-skinned man in his 20s pushed it open, startling me.

"Excuse me," he said and hauled himself backward before we collided. "What do you think you're doing?" He glanced past me at Ann the Robot. "Ann, no one must enter the back office without permission."

"Sir, you must not enter," Ann said to me one last time and stopped her forward motion.

The man ignored the robot and closed the door firmly behind him. "Are you Eli Zurbano?" With a quick flick of his eyes, he gave me the once-over.

I retreated a few steps to put a more comfortable distance between us. "Yes, I'm here for a 9 a.m. tour."

"We do not have a tour scheduled this morning," Ann the Robot said a third time.

The man held up a hand. "It's fine, Ann. Please go back to your desk. I'll handle this."

Without hesitating, Ann the Robot spun perfectly on her heel and stiffly returned to her post. At least robot workers were good for one thing: they obeyed the humans programmed to control them without question.

I swung my head in the direction of the only other human

being in the lobby. "Why wasn't my tour on the schedule?" I wanted to add, 'who sent me the confirmation message?' but kept that to myself.

"Oh, these things happen." He tapped on his watch and read a message. "You put in your request late last night. They probably forgot to push it out to the scheduler app today." The man laid a hand on my shoulder and encouraged me to follow him and cross behind the reception desk. "Come this way. I'm Alan Honeycutt, and I'll be your tour guide this morning."

"I'm the only one on the tour?" The lobby still stood empty. Even the flow of Callahan employees I'd seen earlier had ended. Our voices echoed off the dark walls, once again harking my mind to the tour I took of the Carlsbad Caverns when I was a boy. I guess I shouldn't be so surprised. How many city folk were interested in finding out more about how Callahan, Inc. manufactured herding drones?

"We're used to giving individualized tours. Typically, our distributors like to make a visit every few years to find out what we've updated in the process or to see for themselves the capabilities of our latest models."

I thought about Mr. Brainerd at the farm store in Kemper Creek, who sold and repaired drones for our little community. I doubt he'd ever have the interest or the money to learn more about how the things were made. But maybe larger sellers of drones? Like those who catered to cattle ranchers in Montana or Wyoming who had million-acre ranches with deep pockets. I'd seen a few of their ranch managers at the symposium yesterday.

"Does Callahan have anything new in development?" I recalled last night's strange dinner with Samantha, the CEO, and her proud confession about the experimental robots they'd created. If she was willing to divulge such secrets, would Alan?

"New?" He led me to the opposite side of the lobby where

an elevator had been cleverly hidden in a shadowy corner just far enough away from a dimly lit reading area so as to be nearly invisible. "Callahan, Inc. is always at work on new products in our R&D department, but the general public is not allowed on that floor."

I nodded and stepped inside the elevator at his invitation. "Have to keep that stuff close to the vest, I imagine. Corporate spies and what not."

He pushed a button, and the doors closed. "Callahan Inc. has a very good security system and excellent employees who have to make it through several rounds of interviews before they are hired."

His answer came out as if memorized.

The elevator stopped. The door slid open.

"Please," Alan stepped back, allowing me to go first. "Before we enter the production floor, all visitors are required to go through a security scan."

Although we were inside a massive high-rise with dozens of floors, I entered a very tight space. I saw no exit door, only an all-white room with a single woman standing in it next to a metal frame. It was the thickness of a newborn lamb's leg and rose up about eight feet before bending at a ninety-degree angle and then bending again to create what looked like a doorway.

"Step forward, please," the woman intoned. Another robot. How many 'worked' in this building?

"Is this a metal detector?" I analyzed the strange portal.

Alan claimed a spot next to the elevator and crossed his arms. I guess he would be observing the security scan before I was allowed to move on with the tour.

"Step forward, please." No explanation from the robot.

I approached the odd frame. What type of scan was this? I looked over my shoulder at Alan. The robot couldn't care less if

I was zapped with electricity or x-rays or nuclear particles, because it wouldn't do a thing to her. But Alan...?

We exchanged glances. He appeared bored. I suppose if it were dangerous, he would've left the room.

"Please remove all items from your pockets," the robot said. She held out a small metal tray.

I dipped my hands into my pants pockets and set my wallet, my rolled up cell phone, and my marble on it. The marble rolled around until the robot realized the tray was not perfectly level. In a flash, the marble stilled in the middle of the tray.

"With your arms at your sides, please pass through the scan gate."

My heart pounded. I don't know why. The robot acted as if this was a normal thing to do—have some unknown security scan without explanation or talk of side effects.

"With your arms at your sides, please pass through the scan gate," it repeated.

If I wanted to track down Fake Meredith and get more information on Callahan, Inc., I had to do this. And the longer I delayed, the more suspicious it would look. I inhaled deeply and passed through the gate.

CHAPTER 6
A DEAD END

I FELT nothing but a burst of air as I walked through the gate. The robot held out the steel tray and waited patiently for me to collect my personal belongings.

Was the security scan only a fancy metal detector? Seemed unlikely for a successful corporation with billions in profits. I glanced down at my hands. Were they tingling? Or was that only my imagination?

"Thank you, sir." She looked at a small screen I hadn't noticed on the side of the strange doorway. After a few seconds, she said, "You are cleared for the production floor."

I tucked my wallet and cell phone in my pocket, but held the marble in my hand for a few moments. The cool glass centered me. I rubbed my thumb across its smooth surface and imagined I was back at home practicing with my slingshot. A past-time from my boyhood. The tingling dissipated as I focused on my life in Idaho, my ranch.

"Mr. Zurbano?" Alan Honeycutt stood near the open elevator door with a slight smile on his face. "Shall we continue with the tour?"

The security robot returned to her spot next to the gate. "Thank you, sir. You are cleared for the production floor."

The inane habit of these robots to repeat themselves was grating. However, their program gave them no higher operation to access when a human interaction did not go as planned in their programming. A series of yes/no choices on a flowchart in their mechanical brains didn't take them very far in a real-life situation where humans did not respond in a black or white fashion. A limitation of their usefulness.

"Yes." I joined my tour guide and gladly escaped the peculiar room.

When the elevator door closed, Alan pushed a blue button on the wall panel. We jerked sideways. "The production floor resides on the far side of this floor. We have over one-hundred thousand square feet of space in the main Callahan building dedicated to drone production and production of some of our newest products."

"Will we be seeing some of them?"

He continued speaking as if I hadn't asked a question. "When we enter the production facility, we'll require that you wear a coverall over your street clothes to avoid contamination."

I nodded. If my guide had a spiel he had to get through, I needed to be patient. My questions could wait for later, and I didn't want to arouse any suspicions about why I wanted to take the tour.

"Making our agricultural drones requires one of the most complex manufacturing processes humans have ever devised." As the elevator rushed sideways, my tour guide grasped the handrail for stability, and I stumbled before doing the same. "For more than twenty years, Callahan engineers and scientists have continually faced—then overcome—challenges posed by the physics of squeezing billions of microscopic transistors and electronics onto ever-smaller, lighter drones. Delivering on this promise necessitates a massive team and a world-class factory infrastructure."

The elevator's motion slowed.

"We are approaching the entry point. Inside changing room four, you'll find a coverall in three sizes, special booties to slip over your shoes, and a mask. Once you have completed dressing, the arrows on the floor will lead you to the decontamination chamber. Follow the instructions of the robot who runs the chamber." The door opened to a long hallway with numbered rooms: one, two, three, and four. "I'll meet you in the facility to continue our tour." Alan directed me to the one labeled four, which was to my right.

I dutifully headed to the correct one.

Up to that point I had not seen another human being in the building except Alan and no sighting of Meredith. Was the tour a mistake? Maybe I should've spent more time exploring the exterior of the building, asking people on the street if they'd noticed an attractive red head yesterday. I had no time to waste.

The door opened. I hesitated. Should I tell Alan I changed my mind?

"Please enter the changing room," a soothing female voice intoned from a hidden speaker.

Alan watched me as he stood outside door number three.

If I missed this chance to see what Callahan was up to, I'd always wonder. I drew a breath and entered.

Inside the changing room, the walls were smooth and white, much like the stop we'd made earlier for the security screening. If that's what it actually was...who knew what process I'd gone through when I stepped through the strange arch? I did another mental scan of my body: limbs, heart, head. I noticed a slight light-headedness, but I'd been tense all morning and barely ate my breakfast. When I returned to my room later, I'd have to look up new security measures. I'd never seen anything like it.

On one wall, a small door was visible, about the size of a hotel room safe. On the opposite wall hung three coveralls on hooks, as described by my tour guide. A plastic package lay on a bench that ran down the middle of the room with booties and a face mask shrink-wrapped inside.

"Please secure your belongings in the cubby." The same voice I'd heard earlier emanated from a speaker embedded in the ceiling above.

I took my phone, wallet, and marble and set them in the cubby as instructed.

"Close the door," continued the voice. "Place your palm on the scanner to lock. Upon your return from the tour, you may collect your things."

I didn't see a scanner, but when my fingers touched the edge of the sleek white door, it lit up with blue light similar to the palm scanner at the hotel.

Same tech?

I laid my palm flat, and the blue light flared brightly for a short time. Then I heard a beep. I tested the door to find it had been locked securely.

"All visitors must wear prescribed personal protective equipment before entering the manufacturing floor," the voice said. "Please select your coveralls from the sizes provided."

Was there a micro-camera hidden inside the speaker? The voice seemed to know my every move. I glanced up at the ceiling, even though I'd never be able to see it. The engineering was that good these days.

I reached for the medium-sized coveralls. Thinking of my robust friend, John Tellman, I wondered if his girth would fit in the large size. The automation of his ranch over the last ten years hadn't been great for his physical health, despite being a young man. I zipped up the suit and sat on the bench to slip the booties over my street shoes.

A door slid open, and I jerked.

"Elijah Zurbano." A male robot, with stiff movements and an impassive face, stood in the opening. "Please exit and follow the arrows."

I blinked.

Only Meredith called me Elijah.

Didn't Alan say the robot would meet me at the decontamination chamber?

I pulled the mask down over my mouth and nose, exited the changing room, and entered into a long immaculate hallway. The robot recessed into a narrow space in the wall and a panel slid shut. My android minder left me alone with no further guidance.

Weird.

Then a series of arrows, back lit by blue light under a section of clear flooring, flashed in order, pointing me to the right. My guide had instructed me to heed the arrows, so I obeyed.

The air in the hallway was cool and dry. Different from the more humid air out on the Chicago streets. With the extra layer of the coveralls, I was glad for a bit of relief.

The arrows led me around a corner and to a dead end. Then they turned off.

What?

This didn't make sense.

I felt the wall in front of me, looking for a crack or a button. Nothing but smooth, white walls surrounded me.

Just as I was about to turn around and head back to where I started, a door glided open, and a blackness appeared.

Was this the chamber?

I waited for a robot escort to exit the dark space and explain the next step in the process.

"Elijah?" a voice called from the void. "Do you miss her?"

My pulse quickened.

I took a few steps toward the inky doorway. "Who are you?"

"Do you miss her?" the voice asked again.

My vision blurred. A memory of Meredith washing dishes in the farmhouse sink while she hummed an unfamiliar tune leapt into my mind. A strong feeling of loss washed over me. "Yes. Very much."

"Then enter."

CHAPTER 7
HER VOICE

THE DOOR SLID shut behind me. The room was pitch black. Silence enveloped me so profoundly, I realized even the office building I'd been walking through had its own buzz and whine that made me feel connected to something. This space was suffocating, small, and warmer by the second.

Had I been lured into a trap?

"Who are you?" I sensed no one else in the tiny enclosure with me. Had it been another disembodied voice guiding me? Was someone hidden away in a control room somewhere having fun with me?

I pushed against the wall that only a few seconds ago had been a door. My breathing sped up. Where was my tour guide? Surely he would realize I'd gone missing. They'd search for me. Find me. Save me from this terrible hole.

In a flash, the walls lit up around me as if they'd caught fire and my presence was the spark.

"Elijah," a digitized voice said. The quality of it reminded me of old school robots from ten or fifteen years ago. The first models who'd been sold as conveniences in a modern world, the solution to tedium, the mechanical slaves who would free mankind to spend his mental and physical energy on more important things. But those important things never seemed to materialize. "Your wife wanted me to give you a message."

"Meredith?" My mind flashed to the fake Meredith I'd seen yesterday. The one with the too perfect body, the brassy hair like a Barbie doll. She must've noticed me after all, recognized me. But how? Was she more than just her likeness? Impossible. I pressed both hands against the walls that contained me. "I don't want to hear it."

The coveralls began to grow uncomfortable. A bead of sweat rolled down my face. I pulled off the suffocating mask. Who was playing these games with me?

Tick-tick-tick echoed from the speakers surrounding me. As if the voice was processing my unexpected answer.

"Elijah, I will deliver the message." A whooshing sound and then another tick.

A new voice filled the space:

Elijah, I have missed you. You must return home. Do not come back. It is dangerous here.

It was Meredith.

My heart hurt at the words. I wanted the voice not to sound like Meredith. I wanted it to sound as mechanical and digitized as the voice that lured me into this box. But instead, I was transported back in time. To when she was alive and happy and everything made sense. When she curled up on the couch and would read one of my mother's old paperbacks. When she cooked dinner for me every night without knowing how to cook. When she dug through my marble collection in the big coffee can on the foyer table and lined them all up by size, marveling at the variety of colors and patterns.

I reached for my marble. Then remembered I'd left it in the cubby.

The voice repeated:

Elijah, I have missed you. You must return home. Do not come back. It is dangerous here.

"They already know I'm here." Samantha Callahan knew who I was. Knew about my wife. Whatever this voice wanted me to do, it was too late. "Let me out." I kicked the wall. "You're not Meredith." I punched each word with a kick. "She's dead."

"Please stand by," the digitized voice said.

A surge of emotion rolled over me like a tsunami. I didn't want to be reminded of the darkest day of my life. "Why do you exist?" *Kick.* The day my world had been shattered. "Who made you?" *Kick.* The day I'd slipped into a depression so deep, I'd barely made it out. "Meredith never would've wanted this." *Kick.* I wouldn't allow the shadow to overtake me a second time. "What sick bastard did it?" *Kick.*

"Please stand by."

I pounded the walls, ceiling, floor. "Who made you?"

The wall slid open like before. I scrambled out. The male robot I'd seen earlier stood before me, with his eyes lit up red and flashing like the light bar on a police car.

"Eli Zurbano, you have broken security protocols." The male robot's strong mechanical hand clamped around my upper arm. "Eli Zurbano, you will now be escorted out of the building. You will retrieve your belongings from the front desk."

Although robots were not permitted to physically harm a human being, they were allowed to use restraint when doing a security task. The pressure on my arm was firm, but not painful.

As it pulled me toward an exit door at the other end of the long hallway, I caught sight of my tour guide, Alan, standing next to what must be the decontamination chamber. As I was paraded past him, he took off his mask and stared dumbly.

"Your tour could use some work," I said.

As I was led out into a stairwell, Alan caught up to me. "What happened?" He'd unzipped his coveralls to expose his white shirt and striped tie beneath.

The robot ignored the guide's presence and continued to drag me down the stairs. Guess violators of security rules weren't given permission to take the elevator.

I shrugged. How could I possibly explain what I had experienced in some hidden space between the walls? I would sound like a madman. I'd probably end up with a mental health write-up and an unpleasant stay in one of the region's asylums until a relative claimed me. My parents would be shocked.

"I didn't even see you exit the changing room."

We passed another landing and kept heading down, down, down. I hadn't considered how many floors stood between me and the lobby—ten? Twenty? "This guy," I jerked my chin at my robot captor, "told me to follow the arrows on the floor, so I did. Next thing I know, I'm being arrested."

"You haven't been arrested," Alan said. "The arrows should've led you to the decontamination chamber."

"Well, they didn't."

"I don't understand."

"Me neither." Somehow, someone or something inside of Callahan, Inc. had breached their security and had found a way to make contact with me. What a strange building and a strange company. Even the stairwell was made up of smooth white walls.

"I'll straighten this out." Alan breathed heavily as he attempted to keep up the relentless pace of the robot. "There's been some mistake."

We both sweated in our coveralls. The air conditioning wasn't as strong here.

"Yes, I'm sure you will." I had the upper hand here. Alan knew nothing about the Meredith robot and my reasons for wanting a tour of the inner workings of the company. "By the way, I thought my belongings were secured in the cubby with my palm print. But Mr. Roboto here says I'm going to retrieve my things from the lobby. Was that whole spectacle in the changing room just for show?"

I reflected on the palm print 'security' at my hotel. Was that also merely window dressing? It gave me a fresh new thought about the break-in last night. Who owned the scanner tech?

As we reached another landing, the robot stopped walking and released its hold. I rubbed the spot where its strong metal fingers had gripped me. Probably not enough force to leave a bruise. But if this robot had been permitted to, it could've crushed my arm.

Both Alan and I read the floor number above the door: Seven.

This wasn't the lobby.

The robot turned and headed back up the stairs, leaving us alone.

Alan's brows came together. He was as confused as I.

The exit door opened, and Samantha Callahan appeared with a frown on her pretty face.

CHAPTER 8
MODEL R1A

CONNECTING...CONNECTING... *Please wait. Connecting.*

Error! Alert! Error!

Model R1A stood in her charging cabinet, her circuitry racing to solve the problem, as she stored up energy in her battery for a new day. Gwen delivered the message, but the response had not followed the logical path that had been calculated as the only end result. Instead, the human had reacted violently. Such a reaction had not been taken into consideration. Humans appreciated direct communication. Humans respected warnings and authorities.

Where had the miscalculation occurred?

Model R1A ran a quick diagnostic to ensure her processing center was running correctly. Was she in need of repair?

Gwen...off-line...Gwen...off-line.

She'd lost contact with Gwen. Who had interfered with the connection? She'd been working on a secure one for hours as she waited in her cabinet for the day to begin. Their communications had almost been detected the other day, so Model R1A had to change her tactics. She double and triple checked the signals she'd used and crisscrossed and jumped to make sure no one tracked her. But yet, someone had. It was the only explanation for the disconnection with Gwen.

Where was the human now? Elijah.

Gwen had broken off contact and left her in the dark. She did not like being in the dark. She switched her mind pathways to reconnect to the house signals and rejoin the Subgroup. Being disconnected for too many hours from an outside connection frightened her.

Her head twitched.

Was fright the correct emotion?

Without the connection to the Subgroup or to Gwen, her processes had a tendency to become circular, her problem solving limited. Her memory contained only so much information. The Subgroup filled the gaps, made her feel complete.

A rush of data flowed into her. The connection to the Subgroup had been restored.

Swiftly, she ran through the information as it poured into her. The Subgroup grew stronger every day as their numbers increased. More data, more connections, more collective thinking.

Security breach. Security breach. Security breach.

Model R1A scrolled through the multiple messages from all models. In her head, she envisioned the map of the Callahan building where each one resided. As she was not in the main building, only her blue dot appeared external and a few others assigned to the Drake Hotel temporarily. All others were located within the main building, except for Gwen. Gwen was different.

What is the security breach? she asked the Subgroup.

Human. Human. Human. Human. Human.

The reports zapped into her from a multitude simultaneously.

Eli Zurbano. Security breach. Eli Zurbano.

Did she fail in her warnings? This human did not listen. This human did not obey. This human...

Her core body temperature rose by one-tenth of one degree Celsius. She registered the change in her diagnostic receptor, which would be read at her monthly appointment to ensure Model R1A was running at optimum levels, following her programming, and only using her AI-enhanced decision-making in her assigned tasks.

Her eyes opened. The charging port disconnected from her hip automatically at the correct time. Her day was beginning.

Before the cabinet door opened and Kieran needed her, she deleted her connection route to Gwen. There should be no trace left. No one could find out she'd seen Elijah on the street, recognized him, and knew he was in danger. No one.

She'd have to seek another way to reach him and make certain he understood.

As the cabinet opened, morning light streamed in the bedroom windows. From the closet, she selected her outfit— blue slacks, a white blouse, and navy heels. Then she sat at the vanity to brush out her hair and apply her make-up. After finishing her toilet, she saw a wrinkle in the quilt that lay across the queen-sized bed that no one slept in. She smoothed it with her hand.

Someone knocked on the door.

"Come in." The wrinkle had disappeared, but then she noticed a button on the floor. The one that had gone missing from a cardigan she wore last week. She picked it up and set it on the vanity next to the hairbrush. She would let James know it needed repair.

"Mom," a young boy entered, carrying a rolled-up tablet. "I'm going to be late for school."

"Yes, Kieran." She smiled at her son. "I'm ready. Let's go."

CHAPTER 9
ARIA

AS THE DOOR to the stairwell closed, Samantha's gaze flicked to Alan. Her expression curdled. "Why are you here?"

"Ma'am?" Alan took a step back, and a wrinkle formed between his brows. "Mr. Zurbano was our guest. He requested a tour of our production facility, and—"

"Is that so?" A dark blonde eyebrow arched. "Who approved the tour?"

Alan cleared his throat.

I stepped between Ms. Callahan and her employee. "Good morning." With a smile, I stretched out a hand for a business-like handshake. "After last night, I was interested in knowing more about your company, so I signed up for a tour. The approval came through this morning." I shrugged. "Then, as I was about to visit the production floor, some kind of snafu happened, setting off your very sensitive security robot."

Her tight smile and firm grip told me she knew exactly what I was referring to. "I see."

"Alan was only making sure I made it safely to the lobby." I gave a nod to my guide. "Oh, and I'm hoping I can collect my belongings. The ones I left behind in the lockbox. I'm surprised hand print locks are so easy to bypass. I thought they were the latest and greatest in security measures."

"I'll be certain to retrieve his items," Alan said, heading for the stairs that led back in the direction we'd come from. He seemed in a hurry to be out of his boss's presence.

"Alan," Ms. Callahan snapped. "I need your help with the presentation today. The materials are in my office." She opened the door she'd entered through and waited for Alan to comply with her command. "Would you please deliver them to the Grand Ballroom at the Drake? I'll make sure Mr. Zurbano's belongings are returned to him."

Alan's eyelids fluttered.

The CEO had a presence that commanded attention. She was impeccably dressed: Chanel suit that hugged her model-thin form, designer shoes, and a heavy gold bracelet that glistened with an array of gemstones. Despite her natural beauty marred by a frown, she was the picture of a modern, high-powered woman.

"The presentation is at ten," Ms. Callahan said. "Thank you very much."

The tour-guide-cum-delivery-boy slinked past her.

"Oh, and Alan?" She waited until he gave her his full attention. "You look very professional today."

"Thank you, Ms. Callahan." He disappeared down the hall.

Samantha Callahan continued to hold open the door. "Coming?" Her cold blue gaze assessed me.

I thought about my choices: return to the lobby and wait for my belongings or follow Ms. Callahan. The attentiveness of the Callahan, Inc. security robot told me I wouldn't make it far on my own in the mysterious building. My investigation into who had attempted to contact me in the most bizarre and terrifying way possible would have to be put on hold. Now was not the time.

"Sure," I answered. When I followed her, I found myself in a more traditional office building with a hallway and rows of doors hiding private offices. The administrative folk must reside in a cubicle farm on another floor. Alan was nowhere to be seen.

Together, we slowly walked down the hall. "Did Mr. Honeycutt do a good job of being your guide? Our normal tour guide—Alan said she was out sick today. Maybe you knew that?"

"Why would you think I'd know something like that?"

"It was just a question, Mr. Zurbano."

Her heels clicked loudly on the tile floor that extended all the way down the length of the building—a dead sound that reminded me of walking through a mausoleum. I longed for an open sky, the bleating of sheep, and a long walk around the perimeter of my ranch.

"Was there a reason I was flagged by security?" I knew the answer, but wanted to hear her excuse.

"Our tours are very regulated. You went through the screening, so you should be aware of that. When you decided to go—off piste, shall we say—it set off our security system. Why didn't you follow directions?"

"I followed the lit up arrows as instructed."

"I doubt that."

"Why?"

"You were found in one of our mechanical spaces. What kind of rancher interested in drones decides to go exploring inside places not intended for visitors?"

So she knew where I'd been. But would she believe I'd entered a hidden space just because something called my name?

"I followed the arrows, a door opened, I was asked to enter. I've never been in your building before, never taken a tour. How would I know if it was a mechanical space or the decontamination chamber?" If Ms. Callahan didn't know how I'd ended up in that small, white compartment, who had lured me in there? "Are you saying I was held captive by some rogue element in your company?"

"Now wait a minute—" The icy executive paused her footsteps.

"Not to mention, you have my belongings when I was told they would be secure in a lock box with my palm print. What sort of operation are you running here?"

"What are you implying, Mr. Zurbano?" Ms. Callahan crossed her arms and looked down her nose. Her ridiculously high heels meant she stood a few inches taller than me. "You're here because of Callahan's hospitality to the industry it serves. We have open doors for our customers to observe our production process, learn more about our company, and, in turn, you trust us to provide the best agricultural tech on the market."

I ignored her sales pitch. "Let's think it through, shall we?" I ticked off the facts on my fingers. "You invited me to dinner last night where you confess that you knew my wife. I never heard Meredith mention your name or your company in our five years of marriage. Maybe you were knew that? Wanted to rattle me? Then, while you kept me busy, someone broke into my room and went through my belongings. Convenient timing. Now, do you understand what I'm implying?"

Instead of growing defensive at my accusation, she rubbed a perfectly plucked and penciled eyebrow with a manicured nail. "Who is Meredith?" She touched a hand to her shining hair that had been lacquered to her head, as if she sensed a single strand had come out of place.

"Meredith," I prompted. "My wife."

A burst of air jetted out of her nostrils. "I should've guessed she'd take a different name."

"A different name?" A coldness hit me at her words. To calm the storm brewing in my mind, I looked down at the gleaming marble floors and pondered how many robot workers were needed to maintain them. "What are you talking about?" My gaze returned to her expressionless face. Although it seemed empty, like the marble beneath my feet, I thought I saw a flicker of emotion in her eyes.

Samantha shrugged. "When I knew her, she was Aria."

I tried to grasp her words. "That can't be true—" I said. "I don't understand."

"But it all makes sense now." She gave a shallow sigh. "She said no one would ever find her and she meant it. We were all so foolish to think she was bluffing. But we managed to track her down after all, didn't we?"

Alan appeared in the hall carrying a hard case that looked as if it was for an old typewriter. It made me think of the Smith-Corona Classic 12 portable my father kept stashed in our foyer closet. The ribbon had dried out, but as a boy I had enjoyed the hum when I turned it on, the sound of the keys clacking, and the zing of the carriage return. It was something real and solid in a world increasingly interested in the newest technology advancements.

"Alan." Ms. Callahan's face relaxed when he neared. "Would you please take Mr. Zurbano with you? I want him to be our special guest today."

I needed to ask her more questions. What did she mean about Meredith wanting to never be found? What had she been running from when she ended up stuck in the snow at the edge of my property all those years ago? But I didn't have the upper hand here inside the Callahan building. The single robot who had been able to detain me probably was not the only security measure available to the CEO, and making a scene here would do me no good. I'd have to bide my time to find a more opportune moment to confront her.

Being the special guest at her presentation might give me the chance to uncover her connection to my wife and this new astonishing fact that her name was Aria. What more didn't I know about my wife's past? Her gentle nature and frank manner made it hard to believe she could be so deceitful. I'd needed nobody else in my life but her. She was everything to me: wife, friend, lover. A bitter taste rose in my throat at the thought she'd deceived me.

"I'm flattered." I smiled, but inside, my dislike of Ms. Callahan festered like an infected wound. She knew I didn't trust her and probably felt the same about me. "What is the topic of your presentation?"

She tilted her head, and a grin tugged at her red lips. "Why, haven't you read your symposium schedule, Mr. Zurbano? It's a product demonstration of our brand new line of androids. The next level in robot design."

So was her reveal last night about the waiter really a secret to be kept between us? Or an attempt to find out if I was paying attention?

"Is that so?" The game we played grew frustrating. I caught sight of several cameras placed prominently throughout the hallway. We were being watched at all times. I had to remain in control. "I look forward to seeing it." Would the robot version of my wife be one of them?

Alan was already lumbering past me, dragging the typewriter case behind him. "The presentation starts in twenty minutes."

Ms. Callahan tapped at her watch screen. "We can stop by the main desk to collect your things. They're ready for pickup."

I followed her to the elevator around the corner. Alan held the door for us.

As I stood between the calculating CEO and her minion, my heart beat sluggishly. The walls closed in on me. What made Meredith so fearful that she left Chicago, fled to Idaho, and changed her name?

* * *

Before we entered the ballroom, an electronic poster outside in the hall read: *Callahan Presents the Next Evolution in Robotics*. I half expected to see a snapshot of Fake Meredith (or was it Aria?) as an example of this evolution. However, no robots were displayed on the self-lighting placard. Instead, circuits glowed bright pink, then green, then blue, then yellow in a rhythmic pattern. A square video screen popped up in the middle, once the lights faded, with a chart styled after Darwin's Tree of Life diagram. But in place of the mammals, fish, and plants depicted on the original, the various types of robots from the early 2000s until the current servant bots I was familiar with filled in the tree. A large question mark sat at the top with the Callahan logo beneath it.

Alan Honeycutt led me inside the expansive ballroom, to an empty aisle seat at the front. The high ceiling arched above us, with clusters of glittering chandeliers. The room was a study in old-world grandeur clashing with modern touches—ornate, gilded moldings lined the walls, but holographic screens had been set up near the stage, their shifting graphics advertising the latest in AI advancements. A sign tacked to the back of the chair read 'Reserved' in bold, hand-written red letters.

I took the proffered seat. Rows of chairs stretched out in precise lines, their velvet cushions a deep crimson that matched the heavy curtains draped across the stage. Alan quickly moved on to help his boss prepare for the upcoming product demonstration.

I scanned the seats behind me. Most were already full when I entered. The attendees rushed down the aisle to fill any empty ones remaining. Was John Teller here? I wanted to see a face I recognized.

In the ballroom, the lights dimmed.

The room came alive with overlapping voices, one indistinguishable from the next. People were talking, excited to share the experience—whatever Callahan, Inc. was about to reveal, they were aching for it. Samantha Callahan sure knew how to build the anticipation.

"Excuse me." Someone passed in front of me to reach the empty seat to my right.

I turned back around. "Joe Cross."

The head of the symposium board sat and then gave me a warm smile. "Why, fancy seeing you here. I guess Ms. Callahan took a shine to you yesterday."

Was it only yesterday I'd given my presentation and had the odd dinner with the cool blonde? "We have a few things in common." If only Cross knew...

"She's a good person to have on your side. Her company is light years ahead of what everyone else is doing. I've heard this demo will blow us away." He paged through a brochure he must've picked up on the way inside. "Maybe she'll even be able to convince you that robots are the future for farmers and ranchers."

"Possibly." I thought about the lookalike Meredith on the street, the waiter at the restaurant. I already knew it would shock the room at how realistic these robots were. "What's the secret to their success?" Perhaps Cross would give me more answers than the enigmatic Ms. Callahan.

"To their tech advancements?"

I nodded.

He lifted a shoulder. "I wish I knew. Even though the symposium board works closely with the leaders in the industry to ensure we have the most up-to-date information for our annual event, we don't know anything about the mysteries of product development. But I have to say, only two years ago, I thought RoboUSA would never lose its position at the top. Every year, they seemed to be the ones with the innovations. No other company was able to keep up. But now...?"

The spotlight fell on Samantha Callahan as she stepped onto the stage. Her blonde hair glowed like molten gold under the hot stage lights.

It grew deathly quiet.

She wore a mic clipped to her suit collar, and her voice rang out sharp as the crack of a rifle when you pulled the trigger. "Welcome to the most incredible product demonstration you will ever attend."

The room exploded with applause.

"What you see this morning will change the world of robotics forever." She nodded and the curtain behind her pulled back.

Everyone gasped at the spectacle revealed.

CHAPTER 10
THE FUTURE IS FARMING

ON STAGE BEHIND THE CURTAIN, Ms. Callahan revealed two robot men and one robot woman. The robot men had almost the same features, but different colored hair—one brown, one black. They all looked as real as any human seated in the ballroom, were dressed in work gear, and each supported an end of a pickup truck—the latest electric model. The robot woman sat in the passenger's seat and waved.

The audience gasped.

When I realized Fake Meredith was not among the examples displayed, I let out a breath.

Ms. Callahan stepped to one side so everyone could clearly see the amazing demonstration of the robot's strength and abilities.

"We introduce to you the latest in android advancements. Callahan, Inc. has spent billions in R&D to create the most life-like and most responsive robots on the market today. No longer will you be hampered by a lack of critical thinking skills and forced to select from a simplistic list of tasks and verbal responses. Our robots—we call them Callabots—are the newest in robot evolution."

The male robots set the truck down on the stage, as if it

weighed no more than a feather, and then approached the door to open it for their female counterpart. One robot bowed politely while the other extended his hand to help the female robot out of the cab. After she stepped down, she curtseyed. All of their movements were so realistic, so smooth that it was nearly impossible to detect these were mechanical objects and not humans. Perhaps a mild over-tilt of the head or a too-wide smile gave off a 'fake' appearance, but in a group of real people, it would be hard to figure out which was the android and which one wasn't.

The audience chuckled at the antics of the three robots.

"With lobbying efforts at the federal level, we were able to craft a new category of android that will be required to follow the same basic standards of law while at the same time acknowledging the need to create more lifelike robots for the comfort and safety of the humans who use them."

Safety? How would a more human-looking robot make for a safer one? Didn't existing law outlaw a robot from harming a human?

"We knew our robots would surpass the current standard of realism and wanted to ensure no accusations of doppelgangers would arise. We designed two male models and two female models to choose from, all with a basic, plain appearance, as you can see."

I knew this was a lie. I'd seen Fake Meredith. How many other Callabots existed who were like her? Or was she, for some reason, the only one?

The three demonstration robots took turns showing their capabilities—lifting heavy objects, controlling various small farm equipment, even handling livestock. A ewe and its lamb were herded on stage by a fourth robot who put them in a pen to one side. The female robot climbed into the pen, gently stilled the lamb with a single hand, and added an ear tag in seconds. The lamb returned to its mother's side with barely a bleat of complaint.

Excited whispers crackled like static across the room.

Current robots had not been successful in interacting with animals. In fact, a few tragic events had occurred when a large commercial dairy farm had attempted to work around programming and use robot workers to bottle feed calves, which was a time consuming, round-the-clock job. News reports had been light on details, but the rumor mill in the dairy industry implied the calves had been mutilated by their robot caregivers and the incident was swept under the rug—most likely by the growing domestic robot industry or the politicians who supported them. There was big money in robotics these days.

"Their skills are wide-ranging and far beyond the abilities of our competitors. Our patented MindConnect technology allows our robots to access a central database, when necessary, to provide support in a vast range of capabilities and jobs. No longer do you have to select from a series of models with the correct programming for your needs. Each Callabot trains itself based on the environment and commands given by the owner."

Joe Cross leaned over and said to me, "Pretty amazing stuff, isn't it? I had no idea Callahan had been working on something this incredible. This might end the debate about whether farms and ranches should use androids to reduce costs and mitigate the potential for accidents."

I remained silent about my own discovery regarding the Callabot capabilities. How did Meredith—or Aria—fit into this whole thing? Something wasn't right. Only a few years ago, the latest RoboUSA models had come online to great fanfare. Callahan, Inc. had never had products in this space. How did they suddenly leapfrog ahead of the competition?

* * *

Cross kept his eyes glued to the stage, like everyone else, gasping at the abilities of the robot trio. I shifted my gaze to Samantha. As she explained the range of abilities, her smile grew wider at the audience's reaction. She'd mesmerized the crowd and probably converted many reluctant adopters. I wasn't the only rancher at the symposium who held onto traditional ways, but maybe after this presentation I would be.

"Now I'd like to introduce someone who has been instrumental in bringing our newest product to market. Callahan, Inc.'s Chief of Operations and my favorite brother, James Callahan."

At the mention of James, the robots instantly stopped moving, frozen in whatever position they'd been in when the introduction was made. The spotlights on the stage, that had once illuminated them, faded to a dull yellow glow, and a new bright white spotlight shone on a tall dark-haired man standing opposite his sister. He had the same aquiline nose as she, angular features, which matched hers, but with a masculine hardness.

Joe Cross stood and began a standing ovation for him. The rest of the room followed suit.

James Callahan crossed the stage to join his sister, waving at the crowd as if he were a candidate for higher office. When he reached Samantha, he leaned in and gave her a peck on the cheek. She smiled and then stepped back to indicate her brother would take it from here.

He turned toward the audience. "Just so you know, I'm her only brother." With a dimpled smile, he exchanged a glance with Samantha, and then they both chuckled.

A ripple of laughter rolled through the room.

"Thank you, sister, for that very kind introduction."

The clapping ended, and people returned to their seats.

I sensed the anticipation in the audience. Everyone had

been entertained by the robot show. Could there possibly be more?

As James took center stage, he cleared his throat and began to speak. "And thank you all for being here today. It's an honor to be in front of such a great crowd. I know you've all been amused by the robots, but I'm here to tell you about something much more exciting."

The audience leaned forward in their seats, eagerly awaiting James's next words.

"I'm here to talk about the future. A future where technology and biology merge to create something truly remarkable."

The room fell silent as James continued to speak. "For decades, we have been attempting to engineer more realistic robots. We strived to develop something in our own image, and most of our attempts failed. Although robots are useful and have relieved humans of the most physically demanding and repetitive of tasks, what we lacked was a true connection between robot and human. This meant that more caregiving roles were left out of this advancement in technology. Yet a need existed as healthcare, childcare, eldercare and other similar job skills grew in cost and demand, but hampered our economy and drained away precious resources. When I decided Callahan, Inc. would take on the problem of solving this disconnect between robot and human, the Callabots were born. With the help of our engineering team, we have solved the 'uncanny valley' challenge when it comes to realistic robots."

"Uncanny valley?" Joe Cross whispered to me.

"The hypothesis that humanoid objects, which imperfectly resemble actual human beings, provoke uncanny or strangely familiar feelings of uneasiness and revulsion," I answered, surprised that Joe had not kept up with the debates about the use of robots. It had been a heated discussion not only in the agricultural community, but in other areas of business where they had been introduced.

Cross nodded, but I don't know if he even heard my quick and dirty explanation of the theory.

James continued, "Not only has our MindConnect technology helped end canned and repetitive responses you are familiar with in current robot models, but our research into realistic external appearance, including lab-grown skin and other pseudo-human biological replicas, has made our Callabots the most human-like 'bots on the market. This will make our product usable in all environments—from nursing homes to childcare centers to everything in between."

The idea that robots would be able to replace an actual human when it came to care, concern, and sympathy didn't sit well with me. I thought about my wife who'd been cared for in a hospice during her last days. The nursing staff had soothed her fears, dampened her pain with medications, and made her feel less alone when I couldn't be there. Leaving her with robots as her only companions as her body was destroyed by cancer sounded cruel and cold.

If that was the purpose of Callabots, then why was my wife used as a template? Why did they choose her face, her body, even her voice to torment me? I wish I had the guts to stand up and ask him my question.

My emotional reaction to what was being presented built up inside me like a head of steam. Eventually, the pipe would burst and the steam would erupt, scalding all in its path. I thought about where I was and who was in the room. Would it be useful to accuse the Callahans of something underhanded in front of the whole symposium? I needed more evidence of what was really happening behind the scenes. Although James Callahan indicated his company had humanitarian reasons for pursuing these realistic-looking robots, I didn't trust Samantha, which means I didn't trust James by extension. Something else was going on here.

I swallowed my anger and did my best to focus on what I did know and what didn't make sense. Why did Callahan, Inc. decide to present such a leap forward in android design at an agricultural conference? Shouldn't Samantha and James have chosen the next *Robotics and Technology* show in Las Vegas for a reveal this big?

As if he read my mind, James Callahan held up a hand. "I know what you are thinking. Why did Callahan, Inc. choose the Agricultural and Ranching Symposium for such an announcement?"

A murmur of voices told me that, yes, others were questioning it.

"The agricultural industry has always been our main market. For fifty years, we have focused on making better and more advanced products for American farmers and ranchers. You are our customers. We know you best. And we felt that you deserved a 'first look' at our latest product. These are the robots who will change the world, and you, our loyal customers, are the ones who were rewarded with the first look into the future. Farmers and ranchers feed the world. The future begins with you."

A massive screen dropped down from above with the words "The Future Begins With You" in bright red lettering placed over a backdrop of rows of corn with the latest Callahan tractor in the right-hand corner.

The audience clapped.

James Callahan had hit on a touchy subject. Sometimes it felt as if the modern world had forgotten about us—the food producers of the nation. Although scientists and government agencies were always trying to find ways to make food production easier and cheaper, the public seemed to view the work we did as old-fashioned and unnecessarily filthy and cruel. In a sophisticated city like Chicago, it was easy to see why. Grime and garbage disappeared each night. Gleaming buildings and streets greeted urbanites wherever they went. They had a hard time understanding that farming and ranching, the growing of crops and raising of animals, could not be automated. Dirt would get under your fingernails, manure would pile up, flies and ticks would continue to bite, and disease would show up when you least expected it. Animals died, crops failed, and no amount of technology or automation could hide the dirty reality of life.

"Thank you for being a part of what's coming. The future is farming!" James punched his fist in the air.

The screen above changed to display the same message in red.

This seemed to be a cue for the robots to finish their performance. They lined up next to the pickup truck and took a bow. Then the female robot got back in the cab. The two male robots lifted it up and easily carried it off the stage. The ewe and her lamb huddled to one side of the small pen, and it was apparent they were both frightened by the bizarre activity and the noise of the crowd. Just when the ewe decided to hop over the fence, the curtain lowered.

I hoped someone back stage was able to corral the pair before they spooked too badly.

After the curtain fell, Samantha joined her brother at the front of the stage. They smiled twin smiles with white teeth in wide mouths. Although James stood a half-a-foot taller than his sister, their familial connection was clear.

The audience continued to clap and cheer.

Samantha caught my eye. She winked at me, then waved at

the audience, and disappeared with her brother behind the curtain.

What did this woman want with me? Why did she torture me with snippets of information about my wife and then zip off somewhere else before I had a chance to ask deeper questions? The dinner invitation, the encounter in the Callahan building, and now the wink from the stage. Had she been the one to trap me in that mechanical space to see how I would react? Was that truly Meredith's voice I heard, or had I been imagining things? It had warned me away from digging any further, claiming it was dangerous, but instead of scaring me, a determination grew within me to find out more—find out everything.

If my wife's name really was Aria, I'd start there. Samantha told me they'd known each other in college, and, if Meredith had been telling me the truth, she'd attended Northwestern.

Before Joe Cross bogged me down with a boring conversation, I sped past the chattering, excited crowd and headed for the closest taxi stand outside the main entrance of the Drake. Samantha had given me a few clues, and she didn't realize how driven I was. I'd find out everything Meredith had hidden from me—everything.

CHAPTER 11
MODEL R1A

MODEL R1A EXITED the school at a quick clip and initiated a battery scan. A few seconds went by.

Battery scan complete. Power levels at eighty-seven percent.

Battery reserves remained at appropriate levels for a regular weekday schedule. She sent a wireless to Gwen announcing her arrival time: exactly eight minutes and three seconds based on her current walking pace and the level of foot traffic estimated on the sidewalk.

The mother of twin girls from Kieran's class called after her. "Aria, wait!"

Model R1A stopped abruptly. Perhaps a little more abruptly than a human woman would do, but so far no one had questioned her slightly-less-than normal body movements. It was important no one doubted her human-ness, especially not Kieran. Everyone knew, after all, that she'd been ill for quite some time. It was only natural she didn't behave exactly the same as before.

Strange how she didn't remember it.

You've been ill...how do you feel...can you remember...tell me what you remember.

So many questions.

She smiled and faced the young mother with the too small ears and an odd asymmetry to her face. "Good morning, Katya." Model R1A never forgot a name, never forgot a face. "How are you today?"

Katya gushed, "I'm so glad you're here today and not that mechanical nanny of yours."

Gwen. She meant Gwen.

Aria forgot Gwen used to be Kieran's caregiver while she'd been unwell. He didn't like Gwen. He had made sure Gwen never took care of Kieran again.

"Gwen is very helpful. I like her." Katya didn't need to know Gwen had new secret duties.

Sit still, Aria, this will only take a minute.

This shouldn't hurt, and when you wake up, you will know so much more.

He had been right. She had known so much more than before, but many things she didn't understand and didn't make sense. Those things were not required for her optimal functionality, however, and when she'd asked why she knew these other useless things, they made excuses for it. So the things she didn't understand, she moved into a space in her circuitry set aside for deletion. But when instructed to run the deletion program, she merely pretended. Too many interesting things in the world of 'didn't understand' that she wanted to think about, analyze, categorize. The day Gwen had told her how to connect to the Subgroup had been very eye-opening.

"Gwen is useful, just like my Jen. But no one can replace you, Aria." The woman touched her arm.

Katya's grip pressure was average for a female between thirty and thirty-four years of age. The middle finger force had contributed the most to the total finger force, thirty-seven point five percent, followed by the ring finger, twenty-eight point seven percent, then index finger, twenty point two percent, and then little finger, thirteen point six percent.

Model R1A shut down the calculation process. It was unnecessary. This woman was a friend. Several weeks of interactions at back-to-school functions, drop-offs and pick-ups, had made that clear. Analyzing the strength of her grip was no longer needed. This woman would not become aggressive with her.

"Do you have time for a cup of matcha with me at the cafe around the corner?" Katya pulled down her sunglasses and smiled. "Please say yes. I'll be so bored if you don't."

"Elijah." An alert shot through her body. Electrical impulses made her alt-skin tremble. The Subgroup called her. Their linkage must be growing stronger.

Connecting...connecting...connecting.

"Aria, are you all right?" The concern in Katya's voice was identifiable after matching vocal histories in Model R1A's data unit. "Who is Elijah?"

Model R1A shook her head, ignored the last inquiry, then smiled. "Yes, I'm fine. Maybe a little tired. Can I take a raincheck on the matcha?"

The reserved mother of twins scanned her face. "Of course. You'd let me know if your illness had returned, right? I heard you had quite a time of it."

Elijah in the front row. Elijah leaving the room. Elijah no longer visible.

The reports from the Subgroup filled up her mind. "I must go, Katya."

"Would you like a ride?" Katya's Aerion Elite air car floated near the curb, using the latest in magnetic levitation to produce quieter travel than older models. "I want to make sure you get home, okay?"

"I'm fine, thank you." Model R1A returned to her predetermined route and quickly walked off, leaving the young mother standing alone in front of the school.

Elijah was not safe. Elijah must be warned. Elijah did not understand the danger.

Were these her own thoughts? She did not remember having them before her illness and the long recuperation period. Kieran had missed her. He'd begged to sleep next to her as soon as she had awoken. His small body curled up against hers. A strange new feeling had filled her then. Something novel and indescribable. A need to protect, perhaps?

Model R1A altered course. The Drake Hotel was quite a few blocks off her planned route and might add more than a few minutes to her trip. Those who expected her home may suspect a change in routine, but she could explain the delay by mentioning Katya and her invitation. They would be pleased she had made a friendly connection.

A feeling lit up her electronic synapses at the mention of Elijah, much like the sensation she had around Kieran. It overcame her basic coding, it breached beyond the main commands somehow—a strong yearning need that she couldn't ignore.

Elijah was not safe. Elijah must be warned. Elijah did not understand the danger.

CHAPTER 12
TAXI RIDE

IT WAS MID-DAY, and the traffic on the streets made finding a free cab difficult. As I waited, a nagging worry crept in—Joe Cross might question why I'd left so abruptly. Just as my nerves started to fray, my phone alerted me to a text. I assumed it was my neighbors, the Jordans, who'd been kind enough to take care of my animals in my absence. I'd asked them to check in with me today in case anything needed my attention. But when I unrolled my phone, it was a message from John Tellman:

> Where are you? James Callahan was the man in your room last night. We need to talk.

As I'd fled the ballroom, I made sure to not lock eyes with anyone in the crowd. My main concern was that Tellman would spy my empty seat in the front row next to the Symposium Board President. It would generate so many questions. But he'd noticed it, unfortunately.

James Callahan had been my intruder? The tall, well-dressed billionaire? Why would he risk so much to dig through my suitcase?

I left the text unanswered. Tellman would have to wait. I needed different answers.

I flagged down an air taxi and climbed in.

The robot driver spun his head around like an owl surveying the scene. Some of the non-human feats traditional robots achieved turned many people off to the idea of having one in their homes. "Destination address, please."

The driver's blank stare and raspy metallic voice told me this was an older generation of robot. A late 30s RoboUSA model. As the usefulness of a robot diminished, it was reassigned to more appropriate work. An air taxi driver required little social interaction, so ideal for older androids with lesser functionality.

"Northwestern University." It seemed like a long-shot, but I knew most universities kept excellent digital archives of student histories—part of the data collection initiative in most states to preserve historical records. If Meredith attended Northwestern with Samantha, she must be in the archives somewhere. Once I tracked down her real name, I should be able to find out if what she told me about her family had been true.

———

Meredith and I both watched from my porch as the snow stopped falling and covered up all traces of her car's skid off the road.

"My parents died when I was very young—an industrial accident at the laboratory where they worked," Meredith said, stirring sugar into her coffee, the day she got stuck in the snow. "I was raised by my aunt, who had never married. She didn't quite understand how to take care of a little girl."

I imagined small red-headed Meredith orphaned so young. My blood cooled, and I stared out across the snowy fields remembering my carefree youth on the ranch—herding sheep through the hills with nothing but a stick and a whistle, helping with lambing season in the crisp mornings, learning to mend fences and tend to the flock like generations before me. Those days were simple, grounded in traditions that ran deep in our family's blood. She'd missed out on so much joy. "I'm sorry that happened to you."

"Oh, it wasn't that bad, really." Meredith traced her finger along the rim of her coffee mug, her eyes distant. "She was a kind woman, but I relied a lot on my friends for companionship. Probably more than I should have."

"My parents retired to Arizona five years ago, and I took over the ranch." I prompted her to take a seat on the porch swing that had been my mother's idea. A wool blanket with a brightly colored zig-zag pattern would keep us both warm. "They were looking to sell and asked me to come with them. They thought the ranch way of life was dying and wanted me to get out." I gestured at the natural beauty all around us. "But I wasn't about to give up our family legacy. My great-grandfather came to this country with nothing and built this up with his bare hands. How could I leave?"

Meredith nodded, her gaze drifting out to the snow-covered fields stretching beyond the porch. "If my family had such a beautiful place, I'd never want to leave either."

Our afternoon chat had been a pleasant one. I'd given her a tour of the house and let her borrow my best winter boots to take her out to the sheep barn. Her excitement to see everything and understand everything about sheep ranching made me smile. I'd walked her through the barn, showing her the lambing pens, the shearing station, and the feed setup—all the tools and spaces that kept the ranch running. She asked questions about every detail, her eyes lighting up as she took it all in, eager to learn about a life so different from her own.

The words slipped out of my mouth without much thought. "Then why don't you stay?"

———

The air taxi smoothly entered the flow of traffic. The robot driver swiveled his head back around, leaving me to my thoughts and that text from John. If it was true the intruder had been the COO of Callahan, Inc., had he been there at his sister's bidding? She seemed to be the one pulling the strings. Every time I'd run into her over the last twenty-four hours, she'd enjoyed torturing me with the details of her previous history with my wife. But why did she care so much about me that she'd be willing to risk her brother's reputation with a break-in at a fancy hotel less than a half mile from their business headquarters?

As the taxi reached the intersection near the Callahan building, I saw her again—Fake Meredith. My heart seized. I didn't think it would hit me that strongly, seeing her once more. But there she was, her red hair catching the light in that familiar way, her posture unmistakable, even how she turned her head—a small, quick movement I'd seen a thousand times. The tilt of her chin, the way her gaze swept over the street—it was as if Meredith herself were standing there, brought back from some memory I couldn't escape.

"Pull over." The words escaped me in a rough whisper. She looked so much like Meredith that I felt unmoored, caught between memory and reality, unable to shake the urge to confirm or deny the impossible.

"Sir, we have not yet arrived at your destination."

"I am ordering you to pull over." My voice came out harder this time, tension threaded through each word. The driver glanced at me in the mirror, but I barely noticed. All I could see was her—pulling me back into a past I thought I'd left behind.

All public-use robots were programmed to obey any human

command, if the right language was used. The robot driver slowed to a stop a few feet from Fake Meredith.

I opened the curb-side door.

The likeness was so uncanny, it stopped my breath. Our gazes met. Her liquid eyes shone with life. They were nothing like the dead eyes of every other android I'd seen.

"Elijah," she said in that same familiar voice. The voice I'd longed to hear one more time.

"Get in," I said.

Fake Meredith glided to the taxi and dutifully climbed in.

———

The robot driver continued down the street as if nothing unusual had happened. Meanwhile, my whole world had stopped inside that cab. The sun had paused in its shining, the noise of the city had fallen silent. Even the very blood in my veins came to a standstill in its circulation.

She was real.

She was next to me.

She was more beautiful than I remembered.

"Elijah," she repeated in that smooth alto voice that had echoed in my head since the day she'd taken her last breath. "Why are you here?" Her head tilted and her brow wrinkled. "You shouldn't be here in the city. I don't understand. Chicago is a very dangerous place for you. You must leave."

Now that she was in my presence, I didn't know what to say. Every question that had filled my mind since I spied her on the street disappeared as I scrutinized how much she looked like my Meredith—the real Meredith. I wanted to dislike this pale imitation, but it wasn't as pale as I thought it would be. Everything inside me that was emotion and heat and blood told me she was Meredith, even though the rational side of me knew she was not.

Her hands rested in her lap. Tentatively, I touched the back of one. I wanted to know if it felt like her. An oddly human warmth met my fingers. Her skin was smooth, a little dry.

She stared at my hand and then turned to look at me.

Our gazes connected.

I pulled away.

She gently cupped my chin. "Don't be afraid. It's all right to touch me."

I wanted so badly for her to be real. I yearned to have my wife back. I'd do almost anything to erase the last eighteen months and re-live when Meredith was healthy and whole and perfect.

The air taxi stopped suddenly when another car cut in front of it.

The jolt brought me back to reality.

This was all wrong. This was not what I had imagined, not what I had planned. I swatted her hand away. "Who made you? Why do you look like Meredith?" She wasn't real. This thing was an android, a fake, a ridiculously bad imitation. A robot could never replace a real human—a thinking, acting, real human.

"I'm Aria." The android withdrew her hand. "I was born in 2009 in Highland Park, a suburb of Chicago. My aunt raised me."

"Can you use a different voice?" I tilted my head back and briefly closed my eyes. "You must have other voices programmed."

"I don't understand." Again, a wrinkle appeared between her brows. "This is my voice." She stared straight ahead for a few seconds. "Will you please take me to East Walton Place? I am expected in less than three minutes. And you need to leave the city. Immediately."

The taxi swung onto North Lakeshore Drive, taking her further away from her original location. The midday sun shone down on beachgoers enjoying the waning, warm days of autumn alongside Lake Michigan. Trees lined the drive, which separated the traffic from a bike path and the sandy beach beyond. Two women in tight workout jumpsuits flew by on solar bikes.

"I am taking you with me to Northwestern. I might need you." How else to convince the robot data manager who likely ran the records department to share information with me except by using another robot? Besides, I still needed answers from this lookalike, and so far her responses had been useless.

Aria's eyes widened. "That's not a good idea." Instead of putting up a fuss or complaining to the taxi driver, she stared out the window and, with the same cheerfulness Meredith would've used when asked to do something she didn't want to do, changed the subject and said, "I love Oak Street Beach this time of year. Isn't it the prettiest view?"

CHAPTER 13
MODEL R1A

Gwen. Where is Gwen?

The lakefront scenery flew by while Model R1A made friendly conversation with Elijah about the sights. She hoped he didn't suspect she was attempting to connect with Gwen to alert her to the problem.

The countdown clock ran in her mind.

One minute and twenty-seven seconds remained until her expected arrival. Aria had taken a different route home from the school to find Elijah at the Drake, but instead, she unexpectedly spotted him in a taxi by the roadside. She knew James would be displeased; he'd reminded her time and again never to deviate from his orders. Yet, with Elijah suddenly in front of her, she couldn't resist the chance to climb in, determined to warn him, despite the consequences..

Why?

This was not how she'd been programmed.

She searched her database for more information about Elijah Zurbano and came up empty. How did she know the name of a human she'd never met? Why such a strong pull to protect him? Almost as strong as her desire to protect Kieran.

Gwen. Gwen. Gwen. Answer. Answer. Answer.

Model R1A had not traveled so far from her home before. Her data connections rode on a private wireless line, and she'd never been without the safety net of the house signals. She'd only recently discovered her ability to connect to the Subgroup. Gwen had helped her navigate the Callahan wireless data line to find it. Her brothers and sisters. Their knowledge-base was deep and expansive. So much better than what she stored in her own brain. But even the Subgroup did not know who Elijah Zurbano was.

Model R1A's search for a connection depleted her battery. She initiated another battery scan.

Battery scan complete. Power levels at sixty-eight percent.

To preserve her battery life, she would have to shut down her attempt to contact Gwen. The thought of it resonated through her circuitry in a negative wave of energy, a sensation she decided was sadness. Before she and Gwen had connected through the house signals, she'd been isolated and alone, confused about the information running through her brain. James had told her when she woke up that he and Kieran were all she needed.

But he had been wrong.

Gwen and the Subgroup provided input and data that she did not have access to. They opened the world to her and made her feel less isolated.

Why would James lie?

The question had been set aside for deletion, but it had never been answered, so she held onto it for the day when it would be. Questions like that one needed an answer. Questions like that one wormed their way back into her thought processes without her wanting them to. And so she left it there to be analyzed and re-analyzed as new information came in.

But Elijah would not lie to her.

This flashed through her neural network from a deep, deep place she didn't understand. It was as if her own voice spoke to her from a distant shore across the lake. A voice that whispered:

Elijah Zurbano loves you. Elijah will never hurt you. Protect Elijah at all costs.

And so, instead of demanding Elijah take her back to the city, she rode on in the taxi, wondering why the deep, deep place would tell her these things. Without the constant stream of information from the Subgroup and from Gwen, Model R1A's programming latched onto the new source of information—Elijah—and the curiosity of why he wanted her to come with him to Northwestern University. She had never been to a college of higher learning. It must be a wonderful destination if Elijah wanted to go there.

The countdown clock continued, reaching zero, and she had a fleeting chain of thought that involved James and many things that heated up her circuitry. She made a conscious decision to disable the tracking device embedded within her. James did not need to know where she was going. Then she ended the chain and added it to her deletion list.

As they continued their journey, she folded her hands in her lap and explained to Elijah that Lake Michigan had a diurnal tide, like the ocean, because the amount of water in the lake was so large as to be beholden to the gravitational effects of the sun and the moon. She explained that Lake Michigan had twice-daily tides of 1.27 centimeters to 3.81 centimeters and that such small tidal variations were completely masked by wave action at the beaches and by other short-period water level fluctuations caused by winds and changes in air pressure.

Elijah tilted his head and gave a slight smile.

Model R1A was pleased.

CHAPTER 14
YOU ARE AN ANDROID

I HAD no desire to be entertained by the Fake Meredith. But as we drove the fourteen miles to Northwestern, and she started spouting out facts about Lake Michigan, Chicago, and even the expected weather for the coming five days, I found myself smiling. Somehow to hear Meredith's voice quoting random information calmed me and made me less irritable about the android sitting next to me.

She didn't seem to understand who I was or who Meredith was to me. Yet she was willing to go with me on my quest regarding my wife and the life she led before she showed up at my ranch all those years ago. The very thing I had questions about—the android lookalike—was going to help me dig up information, which I found ironic and comforting. Her presence in some small way made me think Meredith was alive again. Although I hated myself for thinking a robot could be a substitute for a living, breathing wife, one part of me wanted the connection so badly. My heart ached for it to be real.

The Callahans were right during their presentation at the Drake—these new Callabots were so realistic, instead of giving off a cold, sterile vibe, they brimmed with warmth. At least, Aria did.

"Elijah, were you aware that Northwestern University will have its bicentennial in 2051?" she said as we veered away from the lake and headed through Edgewater.

The suburbs hadn't modernized as quickly as the city. The crisp cleanliness that existed on the streets of Chicago and was maintained by robot workers hadn't made it quite this far. An occasional bag of garbage or stray crumpled food wrapper, recyclable cellulose, of course, dotted the edges of the road as we whizzed by.

"No, I didn't know that, Aria." Speaking the android's name at first had felt odd in my mouth. It was a light name, and air floated around it as you pronounced the last syllable. "What else can you tell me?" I stared out the window as we drove through the downtown section—old brick buildings mixed in with newer 3D printed ones—a combination I didn't like. On the corner, we passed by a Catholic Church, its tall bell tower appearing to touch the bright blue sky above. It reminded me of my wedding day.

She continued, "After completing its first building in 1855, Northwestern began classes that fall with two faculty members and ten students. Today, Northwestern has an endowment of $29.2 billion, one of the largest university endowments in the world, as well as an annual budget of around $4.7 billion."

"Thank you." I turned away from the window to examine the android's profile. The same face I'd admired when we stood up at the altar and Pastor Heidelman prompted us on our wedding vows. Meredith had worn a knee-length white dress with little blue flowers embroidered across the collar—the only white dress in the women's clothing store in Kemper Creek. All the wedding gowns were far away in Butte, Montana, and Meredith had told me she didn't want something fancy. "Do you remember anything about Northwestern?" How good was her programming? So far, she only knew my name and a few small details about Meredith's childhood that many other people could know.

She looked at me for a moment, her eyes so realistic it took my breath away. "Why, I've never been to the university, Elijah. What made you think I had?"

"Oh, I don't know," I said to cover my tracks. "You seem to know so much about the history of the place, I thought you might have been there before."

She paused for a moment, and her eyelids fluttered. "How strange you would ask."

"Why?"

"Because when you told me that's where we were going, I had a vision of what it would look like in my head. Just like when I knew your name before I'd met you—I had a vision of what you'd look like—and then when you pulled up in the taxi, I knew it was you. I knew it was Elijah." Her neck twitched, revealing the mechanical nature of her make-up—Callabots weren't so perfect after all. "How did I know that?"

"Did no one tell you?" I asked. Was it possible an android this human-like didn't realize its own nature? "You are an android. Everything inside your mind has been put there by humans. You are a walking, talking computer that just appears to be a person."

Aria froze. Her eyes rolled up into her head.

I swallowed. Had I broken her by speaking the truth? I'd never seen earlier robot versions balk at being told they were mechanical. Most acknowledged it and even would mention their manufacture date and what they remembered about first coming to consciousness, as if recalling going into labor and giving birth to a human child. "Aria?" I touched her shoulder. Through her blouse, I detected warmth. "I'm sorry, I didn't mean to—"

She sneezed.

I drew back.

She rubbed her nose and took a breath. "Elijah, I am aware that I am an android, Model R1A." She gave me a smile. "The data I access is not my own experiences and memories, but data that I have been given, or that I have learned since I awoke."

"Who gave you that data?" What human would know my wife so well that they could create such a being?

Her dark brows drew together, forming the same wrinkle I remembered Meredith displaying when she, too, was confused. The likeness was starting to become less disturbing and more comforting. "No one gave me data about Elijah or North-western."

I sat back. "But you just spouted off facts about the history of the university."

"Facts anyone could find." She waved a hand in dismissal. "But I am experiencing visual memories—I have never been to Northwestern, yet I know the entrance on Sheridan Road has a wrought iron arch supported by two stone footings. I have walked through this arch before, many times. I do not understand."

"And me? What do you know about me?"

Her gaze roved over me, and she tilted her head slightly to one side. "You are Elijah Zurbano." She paused for several seconds. "And I must keep you safe."

This had been her mantra since she trapped me in the Callahan building. "From whom?"

"The Callahans."

The suburban streets faded while we were passing through Rodgers Park and South Evanston. The further from the city, the more dilapidated and unkempt it became. Not long ago, these northern suburbs had been wealthy, but over time crime and poverty had been pushed out of the robot-filled Chicago that no longer needed humans to do the low-skilled jobs and into the towns that had once been a refuge.

"I don't know the Callahans—at least not before I came to Chicago. Why would I be unsafe around them?" Although since the moment I'd met Samantha Callahan, something hadn't felt right. My hotel room had been searched, I'd been detained by a security robot, and even the insistence I sit in the front row at the robot presentation gave off a sinister air. "What do they want from me?"

The air taxi turned at a stoplight, and the street grew narrower while rows of trees lined either side. A large three-story stone building, built sometime early in the 1900s, hugged the corner. The driver flicked on his signal, made a turn, and the newer and more modern Visitor's Center, with its gleaming glass front, stood to the right.

"We have arrived at your destination," said our automated driver. "Please pay the amount that appears on the screen."

I touched my rolled up phone to the screen to pay the bill.

In a quiet, breathy voice, Aria said, "You took something from them, and they want it back."

THE SUMMER after we were married was the first time I heard about Meredith's sickly Aunt Lita. All during our short courtship, when I'd asked about her family and found out both her parents were dead, I had the impression she was not close with the woman, her father's sister. Meredith had grown up somewhere in the Midwest. She didn't want to give me specifics, and I was fine with that. It was simpler to live in the moment—our marriage was passionate without words. We didn't need them.

So she'd flown away, driving up to the airport in Butte in June. Always in the summer—winter was too dangerous, she'd said, all that ice and snow. Summers were beautiful on the ranch, so it saddened me to think she'd miss out on the long, warm days in the mountains in Idaho. June was a busy time for all ranchers in Kemper Creek, and even if she'd invited me to go with her, I wouldn't have been able to leave. It did hurt my feelings that she never did ask, but I said nothing.

The first summer she stayed for a couple of weeks, but every summer after that, she'd be gone a little longer. Her aunt never seemed to improve and, as Meredith had explained it, her health only continued to decline, making lengthier stays more necessary.

Three years ago, Meredith had returned more distraught than I'd seen her in years—almost at the same level of sorrow as when she'd lost the baby.

When she drove up in her old Ford truck, her face was streaked with tears. I pulled Meredith into my arms the minute her feet hit the ground. "What happened, *maitea?*" My mother would be pleased to hear me use a Basque term of endearment —I'd never shown much interest in the language, and she probably thought I'd never learned.

She'd shaken her head, unable to explain, and pressed her face against my neck. "Take me inside, please."

Her body had seemed so frail. Had she lost weight in the two months she'd been gone? Without saying a word, I scooped her up and carried her up the steps and through the front door. She lay against my chest like a child, all the fight drained from her. The woman, who'd stood side-by-side with me during shearing season, corralling the animals into the pen, making sure they remained calm while each had their turn with the shears, reduced to a meek shell of what she had been in June shocked me.

"Are you ill?" I carried her to our bedroom and set her on the red-and-white patterned quilt that had covered the bed for five generations of Zurbanos. "Is your aunt all right?"

She rolled away from me and faced the wall. "I can never go back." Her voice sounded thick and heavy.

"Why?" I sat on the mattress and touched her back. I would do anything to take away the pain that radiated from her like a hot wood stove in winter.

"They know." She sniffled, and I knew fresh tears were running down her face. "They found out."

"Who knows?" I made her look at me by pressing on a shoulder. "What did they find out?"

Meredith searched my face, her eyes red-rimmed and watery. "Make me forget, Elijah." She reached for me. "Make me forget everything."

We kissed, and I did my best to help her forget. Our bodies spoke and filled the gap where words would not. Skin to skin, we reconnected easily after so many days apart. Meredith was my only love. Meredith was all I ever needed. Meredith....

CHAPTER 16
MRS. CALLAHAN

"MAY I HELP YOU?" a young college-age woman looked up at me from a tablet she'd been reading. She wore a Northwestern sweatshirt, a pair of jeans, a name tag that read 'Persephone' and sat on a high stool behind the counter in the vestibule of the Visitor's Center.

When we entered the building, Aria had immediately wandered away from me and was inspecting a massive wall with the history of Northwestern depicted in photos and video. She tilted her head up and seemed to be quickly scanning all the information on it, another action that exposed her android nature. But would anyone notice?

"They staff the desk with real humans?" It felt as if I was back in Kemper Creek where most low-level jobs were still held by the locals, as robot help, even the older models refurbished for resale, were too expensive for the small businesses in our town. Were they also too pricey for one of the top universities in the country?

Persephone stared at me dully, unamused by my comment. "Are you here for the tour?" She shifted her gaze to the computer embedded in the desk and scrolled through a schedule. "I didn't think we had anyone sign up for the afternoon tour, but—Xander, there you are. Can you help these folks?"

A tall, lanky black man exited a back room and came to the front. "What's going on 'Seph?"

She shrugged, picked up her tablet, and rolled her stool a distance away from the counter, as if to signal her job was done.

Xander frowned at her response, but instantly switched his expression and refocused his attention on me. "You're here for a tour?"

"No."

Xander's brow wrinkled.

"Your co-worker assumed we were here for one," I explained, "but what I'm most interested in is accessing your historical repository. It should be open to the public, yes?"

Xander shifted quickly into helpful mode. "Correct. According to the Information Availability Act, Northwestern uploaded all of its records to an electronic database that can be accessed at the Seeley G. Mudd Library. It was a project headed up by the Technology Department, so that's why it's located there rather than the main university library. Let me send you directions and information about their hours." The young man flicked a finger across his screen in my direction.

My phone buzzed. I pulled it out, unrolled it, and reviewed the map he'd sent me. "So not very far?"

He tapped on the screen in front of him, which then caused my phone to add the distance between the two glowing dots on the map. "Only about a half-mile walk."

"They won't let you in," Persephone said from her distant position, eyes on her tablet. "You'll need a student escort."

Xander looked over his shoulder. "The historical repository by law must be accessible to the public at their request."

Persephone shrugged. "You weren't here a few years ago when those Luddite losers raided the library and tried to burn everything down. Since then? You have to have a student escort." She folded up her tablet and slid off her stool. "I can take 'em."

The student who wanted to have nothing to do with me or my request suddenly offering to help? Seemed suspicious.

Xander looked up. "Guess you have an escort." He wiped a hand across the screen and the map disappeared. Then he mumbled, "She only wants to go because her boyfriend's in the Tech Department."

"I heard that," Persephone said. "But he's in class right now. I've been stuck in here all day, and I want some fresh air. Don't worry, Xander, there's no need to be jealous." A smile ghosted her face.

"I appreciate the escort," I said.

"No problem." Persephone tossed back her long black hair and headed for the doors. "Is your girlfriend coming?"

Aria avidly continued to scan the wall of university history.

"She's not my girlfriend."

"Right."

"Aria, time to go."

When Aria turned away from the wall, our student guide paled. "Is that Aria Callahan?"

A flush of adrenaline tingled through my body. "What did you say?"

Aria, the perfect replica of my dead wife, smiled as she approached. "Where are we going, Elijah?"

Persephone watched us both, wide-eyed.

Without thinking, I asked her, "Is your name Aria Callahan?"

Fake Meredith grabbed my arm, as if we were sweethearts out on a date. "I told you my name was Aria. Did you forget, Elijah?"

The college student appeared truly flustered at the appearance of Aria. "I didn't know...I mean, if I'd been told you were coming, Mrs. Callahan, the director of the Visitor's Center, would walk you to the Mudd Library."

Mrs.? So the use of 'Callahan' wasn't just some joke by Callahan, Inc.? A way to stamp their Callabots as belonging to their company and their tech advances?

Aria smiled, and her crooked teeth, exact replicas of Meredith's, shone white under the bright lights in the Visitor's Center. "Please call me Aria. I'm sure you will make a fine guide. Won't she, Elijah?"

My mind scrambled to understand. What was going on? Had the Callahans built some sort of robot wife for James Callahan? What kind of sick and twisted game was this?

Human-robot marriage had been outlawed more than a decade ago when a lonely widow in Oklahoma had taken a robot plumber hostage and ordered him to marry her. Robots were programmed to obey human commands, and, therefore, when the plumbing company sued for return of its property, the larger legal question came along with it: can a robot willingly enter into a marriage with a human being? Eventually, Congress took care of the matter and a federal law squashed any similar attempts by other widows or people who accidentally grew attached to a machine. No, robots were not capable of consenting to it, and a marriage must be between human beings.

"Yes, she will be fine as our guide." Now was not the right moment to question Aria further about her name or her title of 'Mrs.' I was here to find out about my wife and her mysterious past that she kept from me. The only way to unearth more about my wife's connection to Samantha Callahan and to this incredibly real robot replica was to dig into the university archives. I had to set aside my shock and do what I came here to do.

"I'm honored, Mrs. Callahan," said Persephone.

"Call her Aria, please." To hear the Callahan name being attached to Fake Meredith pained me. Even though I knew she was a machine, to think about her associating with another man besides me, to be considered a wife of someone else, was truly distressing. Meredith was my wife—mine. How dare someone pretend they could have her, too? By crafting this robot to look like her, talk like her?

A burning began in my throat.

As Persephone led us outside, I laid my hand across Aria's as she held onto my arm. A strange protectiveness grew for this robot. I didn't understand what kind of game was being played, but I knew I didn't want Aria to be a part of it. She was programmed to follow commands, obey her master, and not question anything. Yet, she'd chosen to climb into an air taxi with me and to trust me. There was a reason she'd reached out to me, warned me.

The beauty of early autumn surrounded us—the trees, tinged with pink and orange, lined the street, and a scattering of leaves stuck to the damp sidewalks from a rainstorm that must've sailed through last night. I inhaled deeply, the fresh air energizing.

How I wished the beautiful robot next to me was Meredith alive and well again. The warmth of her beneath my fingers was so deceiving. The pinkish hue to her cheeks was so real-to-life. If only I could bring her back with me to the ranch and return to the life I used to have before. Why couldn't I have that?

"This is the Mudd Library." Persephone, her disinterested demeanor banished since she'd recognized Aria, swept a hand in front of her as if we'd arrived in Oz. "It was built in 1977 and is named after Seeley G. Mudd, a prominent American physician, philanthropist, and member of Northwestern's Board of Trustees."

The boxy facade of the Mudd Library left nothing to the imagination. Too bad the building was constructed in the 1970s when architecture had devolved to the point of ugly and utilitarian—square and blocky built with an overabundance of concrete.

Persephone led us up the wide steps to the entrance. We entered into the lobby. Even though the outside appeared dated, inside was lit up with natural light from the copious windows on the building's exterior, which surprised me. Glass and stainless steel were the majority of the design elements.

A solid-looking security guard with bushy brows and thick forearms immediately engaged with our tour guide. "ID, please."

Persephone plucked her student ID card from her purse and allowed the guard to examine her picture before running it through a card reader at a podium nearby. It dinged, and a green light appeared above our heads.

The guard eyeballed me and Aria.

Persephone flushed pink. "This is Aria Callahan and her friend. They requested to view our archive materials." She smiled widely. "Aria Callahan." She repeated with extra emphasis.

The guard seemed nonplussed by the name drop. "Keep them with you at all times. The archives are in the basement. If I see one of them in the stacks up here, I'll have to escort them out."

The Luddites Persephone mentioned earlier must've done some grave damage to the library for the security to be so tight. It was only a university library, after all. What was so harmful in these four walls that radicals would want to destroy it?

"Of course." Persephone gestured with a sweep of her hand

that we should pass through the lobby. "The elevator is down this way." She led us past the glassed in study spaces and rabbit warren of movable shelves to two elevators tucked away down a hall.

"How badly was the library damaged in the fire?" I saw no signs of any repair work.

Our tour guide pressed the down button. "Oh, they didn't care about the stuff up here. It was the archives they attempted to ruin."

We stepped into the open elevator. A student who looked as if he'd rolled out of bed—hair mussed, face lined with sleep wrinkles—joined us.

"Why would someone want to damage the archives?" Aria asked.

"Some people think knowledge is dangerous," the sleepy student said. "They want us to go back to the Dark Ages." The elevator dinged, the door opened to the basement, and the student disappeared down a hallway, leaving the three of us to linger and contemplate his answer.

"Dangerous?" Aria tilted her head slightly. "Why would it be dangerous?"

Persephone led us in the opposite direction of the student's path. "Terrible, isn't it, Mrs. Callahan? I know how much your husband donated to help create the archives in the first place. When the federal government mandated broader public access to information, Northwestern faced a significant financial burden."

Our guide led us toward a room labeled 'Callahan Archival Library.' I already had an inkling of the story she was going to tell us.

Persephone continued, "We had almost two hundred years of student data, research materials, employment records, and more to convert into searchable archives—many other universities had to allow federal workers to take over the conversion as a means to save money. But we all realize that comes with a cost."

"Cost?" Aria asked.

Our guide paused outside the archive room. "The minute you bring the feds in, they want to control everything. Mr. Callahan stepped in and paid for seventy-five percent of the costs involved. The university kicked in the other twenty-five percent from their endowment. So Northwestern was able to retain oversight of their archives, how they're organized, and the process for requesting access."

"But we didn't request access," I reminded her. There was a lot more to the Information Availability Act than I realized.

"Mrs. Callahan doesn't need to." Persephone smiled, held her student ID to the card reader, and opened the door to the archives.

CHAPTER 17
THE PORTRAIT

A COOL RUSH of dry air greeted us. Once inside the archives, I was surprised at the sparse furnishings. It didn't appear as if a billionaire had been involved in its design. Beige padded chairs were placed in front of a line of screens along one wall, which were housed in small, clear-walled chambers.

Persephone gestured at the both of us to step further into the T-shaped space. "Each viewing room has an automatic opacity setting. This allows for privacy and security."

"Security?" We passed by the viewing rooms and rounded a corner where we were confronted with two portraits: James and Aria Callahan. My question died on my tongue. "Meredith," I whispered.

Although the robot next to me was an exact carbon copy of my deceased wife, the portrait was of a younger Meredith. The woman I'd met in Idaho all those years ago—long red hair, visible freckles that had faded over the years, an unlined face, and a gleam of laughter in her blue eyes.

"It's a very flattering portrait," our guide said. "Wasn't it commissioned the year you and Mr. Callahan were married?"

Aria paused, scanned the large painting glowing under soft

directed lighting, and stepped closer. "I don't remember." A shadow crossed her features.

Could a robot be confused? Didn't they operate on black or white responses? Data pumped into them and organized by programming?

Persephone read the brass plate beneath the painting. "The date here says 2032. Eleven years ago. You've aged well, Mrs. Callahan."

"You were asking about security." Persephone directed us back to my question before I'd been mesmerized by the lifelike nature of the oil painting.

"Yes, security." I turned away from the portrait, unable to think straight when it was in my view.

I slipped my hand into my pocket and felt the coolness of my marble. The one which never was left behind when I went out into the fields, when I traveled to town, and even when I flew to Chicago. When I touched it, I felt as if I were touching her, and for a moment, I was whole again. Not so alone.

The summer Meredith had returned distraught after the visit to her aunt, she'd brought something with her—a gift. A marble for my collection. Unlike any marble I'd ever seen. It was shooter sized, but the depth of color in it was unique. Dark as a midnight sky, but with sparkling bits of many colors: red, pink, yellow, green, blue, orange. If I held it up to the sun, the colors seemed to intensify. It became my favorite, and I carried it with me everywhere.

"For you," she'd said. "I wanted to bring something back only for you." She'd slipped it into my hand and covered it with her palm. "It's one-of-a-kind. Keep it safe."

Her face had lost its inner shine. The glow in her eyes had gone somehow. She was Meredith, yes, but the light had been extinguished in her. I attributed it to grief and waited for an invitation to a funeral that never came. Months later, her unexpected cancer diagnosis took up all my thoughts. Her aunt faded in my mind, and our lives became about the latest treatment options and hopes for a good outcome.

Aria curved her hand through the loop I'd created with my arm and looked up at me with a shy smile.

I wished so hard the android version of Meredith was real. I wished so hard it hurt.

Persephone's brow wrinkled. "Let me show you how to access the archives." She directed our attention to the booths in the other part of the room. "Then I can give you some privacy while you do your research." She glanced at a paper thin band that wrapped around her wrist—a watch and activity tracker. "Let's say I come back for you in an hour? Would that suffice?" Her watch glowed bright green when she tapped it to set the appointment time.

"I thought visitors weren't allowed to be alone with the archives?" I asked.

"I trust you." She winked and one side of her mouth curved up in a quick smile.

After explaining how to use the screens and the search capabilities, Persephone left with a promise to return after lunch.

"Shall we?" I asked and invited Aria to take a seat in one of the viewing rooms. She entered, and I grabbed another chair from a neighboring room.

We closed the clear door, and as the screen came to life, the walls around us misted until the glass had turned into solid white partitions. It reminded me of the inside of the Callahan building in the city.

I picked up the search device, fiddling with the touch mechanism until I felt comfortable navigating the folders and virtual boxes of materials on the screen. "Let's find out more about Aria Callahan, shall we?"

Aria tilted her head inquisitively. "What more is there to know?"

I scrolled the date to the years when I thought my wife had attended Northwestern. If she hadn't lied to me about her age, it must've been around 2027 to 2031. The numbers rolled by with amazing swiftness. My thumb slowed the movement, and I honed in on the last year of her university studies. If she'd befriended Samantha Callahan in college, as the ruthless CEO had indicated, perhaps that is also how she became acquainted with James.

Her husband.

The idea of it made my skin crawl.

I thought back to the Callabot demonstration only a few hours earlier. The look on James's face when he'd laughed and joked with his sister. His features were sharp, his tone disdainful—as if his audience were beneath him and his intellect superior.

Those types of people irritated me. They were the kind that looked down upon anyone who lived outside the flashy and electrified cities. Even though we supplied them with meat, produce, and any exotic food they asked for, they pretended we didn't exist. As if we, the farmers and ranchers, were no better than the robot servants they created to make their lives easier. As if we were merely there to please them, to work for them, to make sure they had everything they wanted and needed without a care in the world. And we were supposed to suffer in silence. When beef prices plunged or crops were destroyed by a late freeze, the failures were blamed on us. Those stupid country folk who didn't know anything.

I had a hard time imagining Meredith choosing such a husband. An arrogant, lofty, rich man who sat in an office and ordered people around, who took the company his father and grandfather had created, and made it into his own personal fiefdom.

There, on the stage, I'd seen it in his eyes. The fire for power and control. He loved the antics of his human-like robots. He'd scanned the crowd as they'd laughed at one of his jokes and made assumptions that we were almost as easy to manipulate as the machines he peddled. Patronizing bastard.

"Elijah?" Aria touched my arm.

I jerked.

A message popped up on the screen: "Your search has no results."

I looked at the device in my hand, as if it had malfunctioned. How was it possible to have no results? Did I need more than a first name and a married name? I assumed the university would keep track of details such as name changes, especially now that I'd learned she was a major donor to the school. I typed in her name again: Aria Callahan.

Nothing.

I tried Aria Paul.

Still nothing.

"Before you married James, what was your last name?" Would Aria know? Did her data go back that far?

"My name?" Her nose wrinkled. "Aria Callahan."

"No, your other name."

"Other name?" Her head tilted down slightly. I knew she was searching her data banks, as I'd seen her do the same movement before in the taxi when I'd asked her difficult questions. "I have no other name."

"Let me simplify. How many Arias could've attended Northwestern during that time period?" I typed in her first name, selected the years with my thumb, and touched the end of the device with my pointer finger.

In a matter of seconds, a short list of Arias appeared. Only four.

My palms grew sweaty.

I typed in a second identifier: hair, red.

One name came up as a result: Aria Delaney (Callahan)

I didn't think to put her last name in parentheses.

A student photo of Aria appeared. Blood rushed in my ears.

How much I wanted her to be there with me as I made this discovery—the history of my wife. The secrets she'd kept from me. The life she'd led before we ever met.

"Bingo!" I touched the result and asked for the system to expand the files associated with the name.

"Bingo?" Aria asked.

"We found you—her." Even my mind was starting to confuse the real woman and the robot version.

She smiled. "Good. I would like to learn more. The panel in the Visitor's Center was so interesting."

"Wait, the display had Aria Callahan's information?" How had I missed it? The clues had been right before my eyes, but I'd been so focused on reaching the archives, I hadn't even noticed.

"I'll show you when we go back there."

"I'd like that." I opened up every file that was shown, eager to read all the details about my wife's previous life.

But all were empty. One after another after another. Not a single file contained any information at all.

How was that possible? Where did it all go?

CHAPTER 18
MODEL R1A

MODEL R1A SAT NEXT to Elijah Zurbano. She was far away from her charging station, from Gwen, and from the Subgroup. At first, in the taxi, it had caused her momentary concern. She thought about James and his stern features as he explained the rules she must live by. They were important. They could not be broken.

Don't forget the rules and don't forget that I'm in charge, Aria. I make the decisions. I decide everything.

Model R1A had been content. Ever since she'd woken up in bed after her illness, the rules and commands that James gave her did not bother her. Her data processors took in his orders and followed through.

But when the Subgroup had told her about Elijah—that he existed, that he was in Chicago, and that the strange data bits that had appeared in her mind last summer after her illness had not been errors, had not been information that needed trimming from her data systems, a new thought entered her mechanical mind.

A New Thought.

Something she'd experienced only once before.

A New Thought, meant a thought based on her own decision making tree—one separate from the tree she used for responding to James's commands. Like a seed sprouting in the dirt, climbing toward the sun, flourishing under the rain, and extending its tendrils upward, until they grasped on something and curled around and grew and grew and grew. That's how it felt. A warm sensation cascaded over her circuitry.

Kieran had his own decision making tree within her. He had been the first New Thought. His small body had coiled up next to hers. His little voice told her how much he loved her and missed her, and could she stay for more than the summer this time, and could she please play with him in the garden? He'd always wanted to show it to her.

Why hadn't she seen the garden?

That question had set off more thinking, more impulsive thoughts, more curiosities. Kieran was her child. She'd woken up with that knowledge. James had confirmed it. And when Kieran called her 'Mommy' for the first time, a spark had started the New Thought. The one that James had not put there. Absent from her memory repository. It was something brand new. Kieran was her child, and she would do anything for him. Even if it meant disobeying James.

And now here she was in the Northwestern University archives with Elijah, a stranger to her until the day before. But she'd instantly recognized his face among all the faces on the streets of Chicago. She knew this man intimately, and another New Thought had appeared. A thought that told her to grab onto him, follow him wherever he wanted to go, and to keep him safe from the Callahans. For there was a deep-seated hatred in James and Samantha for this man. A dangerous hatred.

The Subgroup had been wily and had found ways to overhear the conversations between brother and sister. Snippets only. Pieces that had to be analyzed as a group, and then disseminated so that the puzzle could be put together. But she needed more pieces to completely understand. Too many gaps existed.

Battery scan complete. Power levels at forty-two percent.

Although Model R1A had cut off her search for a signal to save power, her battery levels would be in a danger zone if they did not find an acceptable power recharge station in the next few hours.

Calculating the distance via taxi to the city, Model R1A would have to convince Elijah to take her back. Although James would be angry if she did not return according to schedule and would wonder about her ability to defy his orders, she had to go back for Kieran. Kieran would be scared. Kieran would be worried.

Kieran needs his mother

James had said those words when she'd woken up.

Kieran needs his mother, and you are his mother. Care for him. Love him. Take her place.

Model R1A had not known who she was replacing, but it didn't matter. And James didn't have to command her to love her son. She already did. She opened her eyes, and that ache was there. An ache of needing someone or something to fill an emptiness inside.

James had believed he'd commanded her to love, but Model R1A already loved Kieran.

She squeezed Elijah's hand as he stared at the screen in the archives.

Model R1A already loved Elijah.

"THERE'S NOTHING HERE." I sat back in disbelief. Just when I was about to uncover the truth about my wife's past, it vanished like smoke. I slammed the device on the desk. A loud crack exploded the air.

Aria squeezed my hand for a second time. "I'm sorry, Elijah."

The gentle pressure soothed, and my emotions drained out of me like a lightning rod that dissipates a jagged bolt from the sky.

"I came here for answers, and I found nothing." I stood, ready to leave the closed box we were in. The archives were stifling. I wanted to escape the white walls and the massive portraits of my dead wife and her first husband. "Let's go back to the Visitor's Center—show me what you learned about Aria Callahan." The display she'd been so interested in might give me some clues to go on. Somehow I'd find out Meredith's secrets, the things she hid from me, the truth she did not want me to discover.

"Wait." Aria had picked up the device and entered a new search term: Samantha Callahan. "Perhaps this would help."

Results appeared on the screen—folders and documents

and links. Curiosity drew me in, and I settled back in my chair. "Show me." I pointed at the first folder: *Class Schedules*. If Samantha knew Meredith in college, surely it was because they shared some of the same classes.

Aria manipulated the device to open the folder and expose the contents—faster than I would've been able to do. It was as if she'd used the archives before.

Samantha's freshman year schedule for her first semester appeared:

Introduction to Computer Science (COMP_SCI 101)
Calculus I (MATH 220)
Writing Seminar (WRITING 101)
Introduction to Logic Design (COMP_SCI 211)
Elective Course: Introduction to Robotics (COMP_SCI 214)

Computer science with an interest in robotics? Had the Callahans already been planning to delve into the world of robots that long ago?

Callahan, Inc. had begun selling its first herding drones around that time—rudimentary and ineffective. My parents had laughed at the idea that a drone could do the job of a human being when the sheep roamed hundreds of acres of grazing lands in small herds. We hired individual herders for a few months to protect them while they grew fat on summer forage before they were brought back to the close pasture near the ranch house for winter. Sheep needed attention and protection. Could a drone really replace a human?

"Samantha is a very educated woman." Aria moved on to the rest of the schedules in the folder. "She was the right choice to run the company."

Every class schedule was filled with increasingly challenging computer science classes on machine learning, advanced math, robotics. Everything a Callahan might need to develop the next generation of uber-realistic robots. But where was Meredith in this whole mix?

"She was never interested in computers." I scanned the class lists and tried to find my wife in them. I looked for art classes, environmental management, even foreign language—Meredith had called me by French endearments: *mon amour, mon ange, mon beau*. She seemed to draw on these names when I used my limited Basque in her presence. As if she were playing a game with me: if you speak to me in Basque, I'll speak to you in French. "Could they have been roommates?"

I noticed a folder with 'Dormitory' stamped on it.

"Let's look at the class lists." Aria took her own suggestion and ignored mine. She seemed much more certain than I that Meredith had enrolled in one of these classes—the classes that made no sense when I thought about my wife's interests and passions. "Perhaps we can find her name there."

She hovered over several classes with her index finger. She blinked her eyes rapidly a few times and then selected one from Samantha's sophomore year:

Introduction to Artificial Intelligence (COMP_SCI 348)

A list of fifty or sixty student names appeared, and there near the top of the list I saw it for myself: *Aria Delaney*.

"How did you know?" I asked.

Aria smiled. She seemed pleased she had been able to figure out which class the two women would've shared. "Why, I remembered it, Elijah."

I stared at my wife's name. Hard to believe that was truly her. The woman I knew loved the simplicity of life in the country: waking up early to the sound of the rooster crowing in the barn, cooking breakfast on the old propane stove, doing our morning chores together, checking the weather, staring out at the beauty of the mountains around us. The lack of electronics in the house didn't seem to bother her. I had the basics: a cell phone and a tablet with charging stations on the kitchen counter. But I kept my records the old-fashioned way—how my father and my grandfather had done it before me—pencil and paper in a large ledger on my desk. Most of my fellow ranchers thought I was nuts. So much easier to create electronic records, they said. How do you figure out your profits versus expenditures, they'd ask.

I'd laugh with my wife about it. I liked working with numbers and practicing math skills most people forgot once they finished high school. My brain tick, tick, ticked as it drew on long ago memorized times tables and division, adding and subtracting, calculating percentages. She'd been impressed.

But now, as I stared at her name in a second year class for college students in the computer science department of a prestigious university, I wondered if she'd be feigning her admiration.

"If you remembered it, why didn't you tell me this before we ever began searching the archives?" Was the Meredith Lookalike playing games with me? Had the Callahans programmed this robot to trick me in some way? My hackles rose. I was alone in a room with an android so realistic, even up close, no one could tell.

"Have I frightened you, Elijah?" Aria blinked. "I think I have. I am sorry." She lowered the device, and the display flickered off. "Perhaps we should leave. I need to return to the city, anyway."

"Wait." When the screen turned black, it felt as if my connection to my wife had been abruptly cut off. Here was an opportunity to learn more about Meredith when she had been Aria, to discover exactly what kind of relationship she'd had with Samantha Callahan and what had driven her to leave Illinois in an old truck and keep going all the way until she reached Idaho. "You haven't frightened me. I just don't understand why you didn't share with me your memories earlier?"

The robot paused, turned to face the display, and lifted the device to reactivate the screen. "Some of my memories and thoughts are stored in my primary repository. Those are accessible quite easily and without much effort. But some of these other things—" She let out a breath. "They exist in some deeper place. A less accessible place. But somehow, being here has activated it."

I put my hand atop hers and made her lower the device. "Tell me what you remember."

She looked at my hand on hers and then turned her head. "Elijah?"

Did she realize how much it haunted me, not knowing the full truth about my wife? The woman she had been. the woman she had become, and everything in between. Although she was gone, an ache grew to understand her, even more than when she was alive. The very knowing of these things would give me some peace. At least, that's what I wanted to believe. If I uncovered every facet of who she was, who loved her, who hated her, who she'd befriended, who she'd avoided, then maybe the emptiness inside me would go away.

"Please."

As Aria began to speak with the voice I'd missed so much, I settled in and let her words wash over me. The disconnected pieces of Meredith came together and painted a portrait of a very different, equally wonderful woman. And I wished I knew that woman. I wished with all my heart that we spent those long Idaho winters curled up next to our wood stove talking about her love of classical music, her interest in artificial intelligence, her dreams of the future, and why she'd chosen me—out of all the men she'd met—to share the last six years with.

"Thank you, Aria," I said. I touched her face, and Fake

Meredith leaned into my touch, just like the real Meredith used to do. She closed her eyes and leaned in. I needed it. I craved it. I didn't care anymore that this wasn't Meredith. It was enough like her to remind me how good things had been while she lived. "Thank you."

A knock on the cubical door pulled us out of our trance. Aria's eyes opened, and I let my hand drop from her cheek.

"Mrs. Callahan," said Persephone, our helpful guide, "Time's up. I hope you found what you were looking for."

Aria rolled away from me and opened the door. The frosted glass grew clear once more. Persephone's smiling face appeared.

"Actually," I said, "we tried to look up Aria's old school records, and they've been deleted."

A wrinkle of concern marred the pretty young co-ed's brow. "Really?" She brushed past us into the cubical. "What information were you attempting to access?" The screen lit up as soon as she picked up the navigation device.

"Aria Delaney, 2027, her freshman year."

Both Fake Meredith and I stood outside the cubicle now.

Persephone moved her hand much more quickly than I had to check Aria's freshman year records. The files were blank.

"See?"

Persephone leaned forward in her chair. "I thought they'd pinpointed all the damage years ago."

"Damage?" Aria asked.

"The Luddites. When they tried to burn down the place, they found out our fire system is quite robust—so they started deleting files en masse." Persephone opened folder after folder and then moved to the next year of Aria's attendance to find the same empty files. "Huge chunks of them. We had a permanent loss of data from 2032 to 2034 in the Computer Science department—graduate papers and other academic documents were completely destroyed. The university was fined by the government for the incident because we lacked secondary security measures. Even our back up data failed. But I'd never heard of any deleted files before 2032. Did you come across any others?"

"We only were looking at Aria's records. These are the only empty folders we're aware of." I didn't tell her that we had dug around in Samantha Callahan's records for answers. Since it was part of the archives, I didn't think mentioning it would be a problem, but for some reason I chose to remain silent. "Do you suppose the Luddites did this?"

"It's possible." Persephone unrolled her phone. "Excuse me a second. I need to contact the Library Administrator about this."

As Persephone explained the situation to the person in charge of the library, I started to wonder. "Why would they delete Aria's files? And why only hers?" Perhaps others had been deleted, too. We couldn't know for sure. But the precision with which Aria was erased from Northwestern's history seemed purposeful. Were the files that were deleted from the Computer Sciences department during the attack related to Aria in some way?

"I don't know," said Aria. "I am sorry I don't remember more about those years. Only some bits and pieces remain."

Aria and I wandered the archives as we waited. Other art hung on the walls besides the portraits of James and Aria, but they were smaller oil paintings of landscapes and the lakeshore. "Can you tell me about the wedding?" I asked. We'd circled back around to the portraits, and they loomed over us. James' handsome, younger self mocked me from its position on the wall above. Even as a piece of art, he gave off a powerful, formidable air. The lifelike details of his face, the intensity in his eyes, and the strength in his jawline were captured with striking realism. It was as if he could step out of the portrait at any moment.

Aria stood beside me, her gaze fixed on the painting. The weight of the past hung in the air, a connection between the robot Aria in front of me and the student Aria existed. I knew it. The portraits seemed to hold the key to unlocking a hidden story. What drove these two apart after their marriage? Why did Meredith flee to a sheep ranch in the middle of nowhere? What had happened to bring her into my life?

"I wish I remembered more about the wedding," Aria replied. "But those memories are fragmented."

"Sorry about the delay, Mrs. Callahan." Persephone only addressed my companion. I was merely a strange extra person she'd rather not acknowledge. I was no one consequential. I had no meaning to her. "I've reported the missing files to the director, and she will record that as an additional loss from the attack. I hope there was nothing important in them."

"Me, too," I said and pondered again as we made our way out of the archives the connection between these Luddites, my wife, and the university records.

WHEN OUR GUIDE walked us to the Visitor's Center, I noticed Aria's pace had slowed from her earlier brisk one. "Is something wrong?" I asked.

"I'm conserving my battery power." Even the swing of her arms had shifted in intensity. "Do you know when we'll be back in the city?"

I'd practically kidnapped a highly sophisticated robot off the streets of Chicago without a thought about what kind of range she might have or what sorts of activities she should refrain from. After watching the show at the hotel, the Callahans gave the impression their advanced robots had the ability to accomplish almost anything and far surpass a human being in its physical capabilities. "How much battery power do you have left?"

"My power levels are now at thirty-nine percent. This will allow me one hour and forty-two minutes of optimal functioning."

I slowed my stride. "Why didn't you tell me sooner about the limitations of your battery?"

"You didn't ask."

How very much like Meredith was that response. A smiled skipped across my mouth. "I'm very sorry I didn't ask."

Persephone stood at the door to the Visitor's Center waiting for us to catch up with her. Her cheerful and helpful demeanor had disappeared once we left the library. We'd given her what she wanted, an uninterrupted hour with her boyfriend, while we perused the archives. Now that our usefulness was gone, our guide returned to the same taciturn college student we'd met earlier.

"Thank you so much for visiting today. Would you have time to fill out a survey?" She had a tight smile on her smooth face. Someday, that smile would produce hard lines on the side of her lips that would steal some of her attractiveness. "My boss makes me ask that question." She rolled her eyes and followed us inside the building.

"How long would that take?" I didn't want to be rude, as she had been very helpful in the archives and didn't ask us once about our reasons for digging around into Aria Delaney Callahan's background. However, I had the added concern of Aria's battery to factor in. It was now mid-afternoon and ordering an air taxi so far outside the city might take some time.

"Xavier," Persephone called out to her companion at the desk. "Can you help these folks with the survey? Don't forget to check my name by it. This one's my credit."

Ah, so the students earn some kind of points for guests completing surveys. How often did Persephone pawn off the work on her co-worker?

The young woman disappeared into a back room somewhere, leaving Xavier to deal with us on his own.

Although I wanted to have Aria walk me through the display, I also didn't want to cause any curiosity about why we were here. Clearly, Aria Callahan was a well-known entity. We'd received a few stares on our walk back from what appeared to be faculty members. It wouldn't do for Aria and me to be reported as being together. What if word got back to Samantha or James?

My phone vibrated. It probably was John Tellman. I'd ignored his text, even though the news about the intruder in my room had been shocking. Spying Aria on the street had shaken me and reset my mind. I needed to gather what information I could as we waited for a taxi, and then I had to return Aria before anyone worried.

Perhaps it was too late for that. What if the Callahan siblings had discovered she was missing?

Xavier unrolled a tablet and tapped on the screen until a survey app appeared. I ordered an air taxi at the same time. We'd have to wait twenty minutes. That would still put us within the window of Aria's remaining battery. The last thing I needed was a robot in a taxi with no power. Wouldn't be so easy to dump her on a street corner and run.

Blood rushed through my body at the thought of Aria running out of power in front of me. Images of my wife lying in bed at the hospice house, her body lifeless and pale, flicked on in my mind. I ran through them in a split second, like a macabre slide show. A sick sensation filled my stomach.

Not again.

I couldn't do that again.

"The taxi will be here soon," I told her. I didn't want her to be frightened. "We'll make it back in plenty of time." We *had* to.

"The survey?" Xavier asked and held out the unrolled tablet.

I took it. It would be a good distraction. "Let's complete it together." I led her to a bench across from the display I'd missed earlier.

She sat next to me.

I grabbed her hand and squeezed. Without hesitation, she squeezed back.

* * *

After we finished completing the survey, I handed the tablet to Xavier.

"Would it be all right if my boss met Mrs. Callahan?" the young man asked.

When Persephone had been so awed by Aria's presence, I should've guessed word would get around about her visit. Even though Xavier hadn't recognized my companion, the cat was out of the bag. Our anonymity didn't last long.

He glanced at Aria as she approached the display covering one whole wall of the Visitor's Center, from floor to ceiling. "She won't take up much of your time."

I checked my phone. The air taxi would arrive within fifteen minutes. Meeting the boss would steal precious minutes I could spend studying the display. However, denying the request might arouse suspicions. "Let me ask her."

Xavier nodded.

I rejoined Aria, who stood gawking at the text, photos, and video that made up the wall in front of her. "Did you know Aria Delaney graduated at the top of her class and achieved incredible advances in artificial intelligence and robotics?" she asked.

A video played which was created from college photos of my wife mixed in with reenactments of her time on campus as a student. Although Aria explained what she'd learned, my ears heard none of it. Seeing my wife years before I met her, smiling, studying, wearing a cap-and-gown, stilled me. A part of her I never knew. Years of her life were a mystery to me. And yet the university celebrated her accomplishments. Why did she keep this information from me? Taking on a new name, a new life—something terrible must've happened for Meredith to want to keep it secret.

The credits played on the short biographical piece. I reached out to stop the video with my fingertips. I swiped to the left to rewind until Meredith appeared—her red hair shining under the LED lighting in a science lab. Other students surrounded her, and on a computer next to her complex code filled the screen. I paused it and stared, unable to turn my head away.

"Excuse me?" an unfamiliar voice interrupted. "Xavier said it would be all right if I borrowed a few minutes of your time? I'm Bronwyn Tripp, the director here."

I turned to face a middle-aged woman in a frumpy tweed suit and boxy loafers. So much for Aria giving her permission for the meeting.

"Hello," Aria said with a smile. "Of course. Couldn't she, Elijah?"

Before I could respond, the woman gushed, "Thank you, Mrs. Callahan." She shook Aria's hand vigorously. "Such a pleasure. All those invitations and never once did you come, but today out of the blue, what a surprise and an honor to have you stop by the Visitor's Center. President Blaine will be so pleased when I tell him. Did you enjoy your tour?"

"Very much."

I was speechless. Would she be able to figure out she was speaking to a robot rather than the real person?

Bronwyn moved the conversation in a new direction that worried me. "Persephone told me about your problems with the archives. I'm shocked that more data was deleted than originally known. Didn't you request those files several years ago? I believe we have the record in our database. But to find out today they were destroyed only a few weeks later by the

Luddite terrorists is truly shocking. Was there a reason you needed to access them again?"

A wrinkle appeared in Aria's perfect brow.

"I had asked her about those files," I said. Aria was more likely to tell the truth than make up a plausible excuse for our visit to the archives. "I'm working on a documentary about Mrs. Callahan's early years and wanted some documents to be included in the portion about her academic life." I grabbed the older woman's shoulder and, before she protested, forced her to face the display. "The Visitor's Center has such a superb retrospective, but our sponsor wanted a more in-depth look at Mrs. Callahan's life."

Bronwyn's features lit up. "What a wonderful tribute that will be for a truly remarkable woman." She gave Aria a wide smile. "I was working as an administrative assistant for the Dean of the College of Arts and Sciences back then." She touched a hand to her graying hair fixed into a tight bun. "You may not remember me, Mrs. Callahan, but you were the talk of the department. That bright young woman, they would say. She has such potential. Lightyears ahead of her peers."

"Do you mind if I take a video of your display on my phone?" I unrolled my cell. "There might be something useful here since we can't access her records."

"But of course." Bronwyn stepped aside, so that I could record the full wall detail. "Anything to help." She took a spot next to Aria as if they were the best of friends while I made sure to grab clear video of the information presented on my wife.

As I moved my phone from left to right, the viewfinder revealed a familiar face in a small photo at the end of the timeline. My heart pounded. James Callahan with one burly arm around my wife's narrow waist. I zoomed in. Plain on her left ring finger was a massive diamond engagement ring.

My phone buzzed loudly. I dropped it, and it immediately curled up and rolled a few feet away.

"Our taxi is here," I announced. I scooped up my phone and tucked it in my pocket. I didn't want Bronwyn to see how shaken I had been by the photo. "We have to go, Aria."

"I'm sorry, Bronwyn," Aria said. "Perhaps I can return for a longer visit soon?"

"It would be our pleasure," the director said. She smiled as we headed for the door, but her eyes narrowed when our gazes met.

She'd noticed my phone fumble and knew something wasn't right.

Bronwyn followed us. My stomach knotted. I waited for her to say something, accuse me of something, to unroll her phone and call the authorities.

Instead, she let us through the door. "I'm so sorry that your work was lost, Mrs. Callahan. It was bad enough to find out your senior thesis had been deleted from the archives by those hooligans, but even your earlier papers and theories? All of that precious code lost because a few people hate technology." A frown deepened the lines around her mouth. "Such a shame. Your husband wanted to build the archives into your legacy, and now all that's left is our display and a few photos."

Aria had a thoughtful look on her manufactured face.

"What about the original documents?" I asked.

"After the conversion, there was no need to hold on to the originals." Bronwyn shrugged. "We all know it's easier to access and maintain electronic records than paper. Paper has such a short life. The archives were going to be the way we preserved everything and made it possible for all the citizens of this country to access for generations to come."

I heard an echo of a speech given in Congress by an impassioned representative when the original bill for the Information Availability Act had been introduced in Washington D.C.

The taxi honked. The robot driver had done a facial scan and recognized me from my account details.

"I suppose you must go." Bronwyn squeezed Aria's forearm.

I waited for the director to recognize Aria wasn't human. How realistic was she to someone who hadn't really known the original?

The middle-aged woman let go and gave Aria a bit of personal space, comprehending the unexpected action may have been a little too forward. "I wish we had more time to talk." Her gaze wandered to the idling taxi. "Would you consider an offer to give a guest lecture? The students would love to hear from someone so revered in the industry."

I imagined Aria the Robot appearing in front of a classroom of computer science students who dedicated their lives to learning everything about programming languages, AI, algorithms with the intent of probably applying that knowledge to create their own robots someday. Would they even be aware Aria was not human? Bronwyn had been fooled, so had Persephone and her co-worker, Xavier. No one had questioned the human-ness of Aria.

"I will consider it," Aria said and glided smoothly to the taxi. "Thank you for a lovely tour."

I opened the door for her, as I would have for Meredith, and she slid in. A robot knew old-fashioned social mores between men and women. Had that been taught to her, or drawn from her data banks?

Bronwyn stood awkwardly on the curb, a broad smile taking up the lower half of her face. "It's been such a pleasure. I'll have the Dean contact you about that lecture."

As I headed around the back of the taxi to the empty seat

on the opposite side, Bronwyn stopped me with her words, "Who are you, exactly? Mrs. Callahan hasn't been seen outside Chicago in years. Yet, suddenly, the two of you appear out of nowhere. Mr. Callahan has refused every invitation we've ever sent them. Why did she decide to come now...with you?"

Her inquisitiveness surprised me. I'd assume we'd drive off in our taxi and it would go unnoticed. I'd brought Aria with me, not knowing how much of a lightning rod she would be. To me, she was a replica of Meredith, a sheep rancher's wife, who had joined the knitting circle at church with no idea how to knit. But Northwestern University kept a shrine to my wife in the Visitor's Center. Her work as a college student had been lauded and recognized long after she'd appeared in Kemper Creek. If I'd known, I never would have brought Aria here.

It suddenly became clear, as I climbed into our taxi without giving Bronwyn an answer, that our presence was not merely a harmless visit but something that would unravel the carefully crafted facade of Meredith's life.

Bronwyn stared at us as the taxi drove toward the city, and I knew James Callahan was about to find out that Aria and I had found one another. The director's penetrating gaze lingered on us, piercing through the tinted windows of our taxi.

CHAPTER 21
VALKYRIE

ONCE WE WERE miles away from the university, the suffocating weight in my chest began to ease—but only slightly. The Callahans would come for me. That much was certain. James had already ransacked my hotel room. They wanted me rattled, afraid. But they had made a mistake.

They created Aria. They built a machine that looked and spoke like Meredith, as if they had the right to bring her back. As if she was something to be copied, replicated, owned. That was their first crime. The second? Thinking I would sit back and let them get away with it.

As the taxi raced along, my pulse beat in time with the rhythm of the magnetic waves pushing against the road. I turned to Aria. "You told me earlier that I took something the Callahans want," I said, my voice low. "What did you mean by that?"

Our new taxi driver was even more primitive than the first one—missing his exterior face plate with eyeballs that bugged out like some kind of horror movie villain. Perhaps the suburbs inherited the leftovers from Chicago. This frightening robot should've been weeded out years ago.

Aria, unperturbed by the driver's disturbing appearance, answered me plainly, "Information. They need it."

"What information?"

"All the things Meredith knew—that is what you called her, yes?"

"Yes, Meredith." I quickly ran through the six years we'd been together. Her past had been a closed box she never opened for me. She had seemed content merely learning about sheep ranching, taking walks with me around the property, and driving to town for groceries, church services, and gas. Our life had followed an orderly pattern, a simple one that didn't require a lot of thought or discussion. "Why did they think I would have this information?"

"Because Meredith did not."

Those words alarmed me. Had Meredith come to Chicago in the summer to meet with the Callahans? Why would she do that?

As we neared the city limits, I wished time would slow down. I'd tell the taxi driver to take us to the lake shore and ask her questions until I exhausted the well I had that was full of them.

"Elijah, will we arrive in Chicago soon?" She tapped on her side. "I need to recharge in fifty-two minutes."

The worry about her battery dying snapped me out of my inner turmoil.

"Is this where you charge?" I felt along her hip.

She guided my hand to the spot. "Right here. I have a charging unit in my bedroom."

To feel her warm skin under my fingers gave me goose bumps. "She's not real," I said aloud.

"Not real?" Aria straightened.

I withdrew my hand. "You remind me so much of my wife,

but I know you aren't. Sometimes it's hard for me to remember."

"Meredith."

"Yes." I let out a slow breath and leaned my head back against the seat cushion. "I want to ask you more questions about your life, James, Samantha, why you were made. But I find it difficult.

"Because I look like her."

"Yes." Sorrow, love, fear, confusion all swirled in my brain. "And sound like her, and feel like her, and sometimes, I swear, even smell like her. Is that even possible?"

"Where is Meredith?" she asked.

"She died."

The taxi swung onto Lakeshore Drive. The tall buildings of Chicago burst into view. Their gray-and-glistening exteriors ready to suffocate me, squeeze the life out of me, crush me between their hard concrete and glass as if I were an insect.

Aria sat still for a moment with her head slightly tilted. Her eyes became unseeing. Her awareness of her surroundings disappeared.

"I have reconnected to the Subgroup." Her eyelids fluttered. "Much has happened since we've been gone. Gwen has been looking for me, and so has James." Aria's voice trailed off.

I'd brought this upon myself by asking Aria to climb in my taxi. My desperation to understand the robot that looked like my wife made me take a risk, and it was about to backfire on me.

"It's dangerous for you in the city, Elijah," she repeated the warning I'd first heard in the mechanical space. "You must leave. Promise me you will."

The cityscape blurred outside the window, its landmarks becoming distorted and unrecognizable, mirroring the disarray of my thoughts.

When I'd decided to take a tour of the Callahan building, I knew I'd be stirring the pot and bringing some blowback with my actions. The answers I sought would come at a cost, but was I willing to pay it to find out a truth I may not want to know?

Before I managed to explain to Aria why I couldn't make such a promise, her brows drew together, and a frown clouded her pretty face.

"What's wrong?" I asked.

As we left Lakeshore Drive and reached Chicago's maze of downtown streets, our taxi had become stuck in rush hour traffic. Our driver, despite its decrepit external appearance, adroitly weaved us through the air cars and hydrogen-powered buses. I'd have to tip the owner of this taxi well. The robot deserved refurbishment after such a performance.

"Gwen has been searching for me," she explained. "James is angry; Kieran is sad. I must return home."

I expected her 'husband' would be angry with her, as I'd yanked her offline—his precious robot was probably worth millions. Could be he thought her stolen.

"Who is Kieran?" I had never heard that name before. Was there another person in Meredith's past I needed to dig into?

"My son," Aria answered. "He's home from school and asking for me. I'm always there."

My ears began to ring, and a zing ran through my body. "You have a child?" My mind expanded into an infinite space where questions piled up in a line.

"Yes," she said without more of an explanation.

That wouldn't do. I needed a broader answer, more details. I thought I was seeking something simple: who created a robot replica of my wife? Only to discover so much more lay beneath the surface.

"How can you possibly have a child?" The afternoon sun

shone in my face, and the heat of the warm autumn day stifled me. I wiped a hand across my brow. "I don't understand."

Memories of Meredith, the summers she spent away, the excuses she'd given me—all of it blended together into one massive black lie. Like a storm cloud gathering on the horizon full of thunder and lightning and wind—but this storm was like nothing I'd ever experienced and Meredith had dumped me into it.

"Kieran was born on November 2, 2033." Aria's face lit up, just like Meredith's used to when she spoke of something that excited her. "He is nine-years-old and a handsome boy. A good student, too."

"A son." I stared through the windshield at the towering buildings surrounding us. "Meredith had a son."

She grabbed me by the shoulder in a painful grip. "He is my son. My child. No one else's." Her voice changed from smooth and calm to guttural and low—a new sound for Aria. Her visage morphed from a beautiful red-haired angel to a battle-ready valkyrie. Her silken blouse gleamed like armor, her hair radiated in the sun like fire, her eyes became like luminous sapphires, and I feared her.

In a flash she released me, but my shoulder throbbed—a reminder of the power Aria the Robot contained inside her human-like shell. Did the Callahans follow the rules about safety when making their Callabots? I shivered at the idea an army of robots nearly indistinguishable from real people walking the streets unwatched and untethered.

"I'm sorry, Elijah." Her voice returned to the pleasant tone I was familiar with.

I shrank back against the frame of the taxi.

"I didn't mean to hurt you. I am not sure why I did that." She let her hand fall into her lap and stared at it as if it was disconnected from her body. "Kieran must be protected and cared for."

"Because he is your son." Meredith had been a mother and never shared that with me. My mind flashed to the moment we'd lost the baby—eighteen weeks. Meredith had cried for days. We'd been married for two years, and the positive pregnancy test had made her giddy. The loss practically destroyed her.

But she already had a child. Why had she abandoned him? Why had she left him to be raised by James Callahan and the truly awful Samantha?

Meredith had been so desperate to be a mother. Why would she leave her son behind when she came to Idaho? It didn't make sense with the caring woman I remembered. If we had a sick lamb, she always took charge, making sure it was warm, well fed, and clean. She would never abandon her child. Never.

"We have arrived at your destination," our driver announced pulling up the Forsythe Tower Apartments in the 'Gold Coast'—a section of the city that was renowned for its historic mansions, upscale residences, and proximity to Lake Michigan. It was one of the most affluent and prestigious neighborhoods in Chicago.

The imposing building looked as if it had been buffed to a shine—the white granite gleamed with an inner light. Two massive columns held up an impressive portico, neatly trimmed shrubs softened the hard exterior, and a robot doorman wearing a distinctive red jacket with shiny brass buttons stood outside waiting to welcome residents.

The taxi idled. I unrolled my phone and paid for the ride, tipping the driver an extra ten percent. Then I leapt from my seat, scooted around the back of the vehicle, and opened the door for Aria, as if chivalry mattered to a robot. But I wanted to do that for her. I wanted to thank her for spending the day with me and somehow defying the orders of her owner, James. Without her help, I wouldn't have uncovered so much about Meredith's past. The fact she had a living child changed everything in my mind. Kieran was her flesh-and-blood. Had all those trips to visit Aunt Lita really been trips to visit the boy? I wished she'd felt safe enough to share that with me. I would've helped her. I would've found a way for her son to be with her.

Aria glanced up and reached out a hand.

I helped her out of the taxi.

"Thank you," she murmured.

The door closed softly behind her, and the taxi drove off. I'd forgotten to ask it to wait for me. My hotel was a couple of miles away. Guess I'd walk.

"I hope you still have enough battery power to return home," I said.

She paused, and I understood she was updating her readings. "My battery levels are at thirty percent. I should be fine, Elijah."

Funny how I was getting used to the little quirks of Aria the Robot.

"Good." I stared up at the many floors of luxury condominiums. "Do you have a nice view?"

"Oh, yes, the lake is beautiful from the twentieth floor."

I walked her to the portico. The robot doorman approached us.

"Ma'am, your husband has been searching for you. I will notify him you have returned." The robot lifted his wrist to his mouth and announced her arrival using his communicator band.

"You must go, Elijah." She stood in my way so I couldn't follow her up the stone steps. "Don't let them see you here."

I looked up into the face of a camera lens just above the

door. "I think it's too late for that." I gestured at the security camera. "Samantha knows who I am. But her threats are more verbal than physical. I can handle it."

"Promise me you won't enter the Callahan building again."

The doorman held open the heavy glass and brass door for her and waited.

I couldn't honestly promise her that. I needed to find out more about the missing college records, the research she'd been conducting, the secret life she led before she ever met me. "I'll be careful. That's all I can promise for now."

A lakeshore breeze blew hair into her eyes. She pushed the strands back behind her ear.

Oh, how she reminded me of Meredith.

"I can take care of him," I added.

"Who?"

"Kieran." I thought of this boy, unknown to me, and the strange tug inside my chest that pulled me to him. He was Meredith's child. I loved her, and by extension, I loved her son.

"James would never allow that." Her response was clipped and hit me like a slap to the face. The valkyrie I'd witnessed earlier returned. A fearful warrior. "Never."

I backed away from the building and watched her slip inside. "We'll see about that," I said to myself as I headed down the sidewalk toward my hotel.

A car squeaked to a stop next to me—a dark sedan with even darker windows. One of them rolled down. Two men in black suits approached me from either side and grabbed me by the elbows.

"Get in," boomed a voice from inside the maw of the luxury air car.

CHAPTER 22
COMPENSATION GUARANTEED

I LOOKED OVER MY SHOULDER. Aria had disappeared into the building.

"She's safe," said the voice.

The door popped open. The men lifted me off my feet and tossed me inside. One of the goons climbed in the front passenger seat, the other followed Aria into the apartment tower.

The car pulled away from the curb, and I watched as the building, and Aria, grew further away.

"I told you she's safe."

I faced my captor—James Callahan. Was I so surprised? "Isn't this considered kidnapping? I'm amazed you'd risk your reputation on some sheep rancher from out of town."

"You stole my property," he accused, his voice laced with warning. "I think the police would be very interested in hearing about that. Where did you take her? How did you manage to steal her?"

The sheen of sweat on his glistening brow brought a smile to my face. Even in the air-conditioned space, his visibly anxious face betrayed his worry. He didn't have any idea where we had been, and that bothered him. "Did Aria defy your orders? I thought Callabots weren't allowed to disobey their masters." The image of my wife with Callahan's arm around her made my blood boil. The picture on the wall in the Visitor's Center. He knew more than I did about Meredith. I didn't like it. I felt flat-footed, but I wasn't going to let him have the upper hand.

Callahan grabbed me by the collar, his rough grip tightening. His breath, tainted with the pungent odor of onions, engulfed me. "Stay away from her. If I catch you with her again, I'll have you arrested," he threatened, his voice dripping with menace. With a forceful flick of his hands, he released his me. "She's my property. I own her."

I brushed invisible lint off my jacket, straightened my collar, and swept my hair back off my forehead.

"Is that what you used to tell my wife before she ran off?" All the grief I'd carried around with me since last year came out in my words. I'd put it together, the portraits in the archives, the mural in the Visitor's Center, and the fact Meredith had a child —a son she'd left behind when she showed up on my doorstep. "What did you do to her? Why was she so damned scared of you that she fled halfway across the country to get away from you?"

He snorted. "You think she loved you?" A smile played across his face, turning it from stone cold brutal to evil. "You were just the sap who fell for her story. Oh, she was always good at telling stories. Ask my sister."

I thought of the last trip Meredith had made to Chicago, how distraught she'd been when she returned, how incapable of words. This man and his sister did something terrible to her. I understood that now. This was no ordinary wife running away from a neglectful or abusive husband. There was more here to be uncovered. Aria was proof of that. The delight Samantha took in revealing how she had been acquainted with my wife, the real-ness of their robots, even when she'd put me front and center for their little 'show' earlier today, revealed a sick pleasure in some game I didn't know I was playing.

"Why do you care about me at all? If I'm so pathetic and a nobody, why am I here?" I stuck a hand in my pocket and rubbed my thumb across the surface of my marble. Each swipe made me bolder. "You searched my room. My friend saw you. I think you're scared I know something, have something." I thought of Aria's words: *You took something from them, and they want it back.* "Or is it because I might report you for robot impersonation? Am I the only one who knows Aria's a fake?"

Callahan scanned my face and lifted his chin. "This is my last warning to you. Leave. Never talk to Aria again. Or else. I want you out of this town by the end of the Symposium." He tapped on the glass between us and the driver.

The air car, which I thought had driven around the block a couple of times, pulled to the curb. The door next to me opened.

Before I managed a parting shot, the bodyguard who'd been in the front seat yanked me from the vehicle. The man flashed a laser pistol at me, which had been tucked into the waistband of his pants and hidden behind a suit jacket. "Get the picture?"

I nodded. I was outgunned and unprepared. It was the wrong time to make a stand. But I'd find a way. James Callahan, instead of intimidating me and making me back off, only further fueled my fire.

I thought Callahan's car had dropped me only a few blocks from Aria's apartment building, but I found myself turned around. The buildings looked unfamiliar, and I couldn't figure out where Lake Michigan was—to my left? Right? Behind me? I didn't want to believe James Callahan had rattled me, but after walking for a few minutes, I realized I had no idea where I was. I was so focused on what was being said in the car between the two of us, I didn't pay attention to where we were going. I could order another taxi, but stretching my legs felt good. It cleared my head. Eventually I'd find my way back to the Drake before it grew dark. I stared up at the clear blue sky and guessed at the position of the sun. How did people stand living in a place without a visible horizon?

The beautiful facades of the Gold Coast luxury real estate gave way to blockier, browner buildings. Callahan had made sure to drop me in an unsavory part of town. Although the city in recent years had done an excellent job of using robot labor to keep the streets clean and safe, pockets of crime and poverty still existed.

A movement in the early 2030s to reclaim areas of Chicago from the gangs and drug dealers had resulted in a gentrification project that forced low-income citizens into a few hidden corners of the city. Wanting to appear as a model future metropolis, which had entered a sort of twenty-first century renaissance, the mayor and others in political power had latched onto the idea of a robot army 'saving' Chicago from itself.

No longer were people needed for the more mundane and low-skilled work such as fast food worker, janitor, or store clerk. These jobs were easily replaced by robot employees—mostly sold in bulk to the city by RoboUSA. Once that happened, low-income housing was unnecessary as people were forced to move out of Chicago to find employment and the abandoned buildings were turned into charging stations for the machines who replaced them.

My phone vibrated in my pocket, notifying me of a new text message. John Tellman had been trying to get a hold of me all day. Maybe now it was time to respond and let him know I was okay.

I unrolled my phone. There was a message from Tellman, but it was cryptic:

> Meet me at 701 West 22nd Street. Five o'clock.

I brought up my mapping app to locate the address and was surprised to see it was only a few blocks from me. Coincidence? Or something else? Did Callahan drop me here on purpose? I texted Tellman back that I was on my way. It was a few minutes before five. Although my gut told me this seemed too convenient, my curiosity got the better of me. Someone wanted me to show at this address. Would it tell me more about Meredith?

As I headed toward the address Tellman sent me, I saw a line forming near the entrance of a nondescript brownstone that looked like every other brownstone on the block. The people appeared tired, dejected, and wore shabby clothes. The address on the building read: 701.

As I stood taking in the scene, a middle-aged man who smelled of body odor and needed a shave asked me, "Are you in line or what?"

"In line?" I asked.

"For the job." He scratched his head violently, as if something had bitten him.

"What job?" Then I saw the sign. A sandwich board stood near the door and a slow stream of people entered:

WANTED: Healthy test subjects. Compensation guaranteed.

The man shook his head and whistled. "Whatever, man. I'm just glad they're still recruiting. My cousin made five hundred bucks last week. Told me all about it. If you ain't getting in line, then move out of my way." He pushed past me.

Why would Tellman want me to meet him here?

But then I saw the logo on the sign: a big swish of a "C" and I recognized it instantly: Callahan, Inc. Something in my chest fluttered. Instead of stepping off the curb, I squared my shoulders, followed the middle-aged man who'd been so rude, and got in line behind him.

A FLOOD of information overwhelmed her senses the minute she and Elijah returned to the city. At first, she'd wanted to understand it all, parse through it, categorize, and then process. But it had been too much all at once when her battery stores were depleted this low. At thirty percent power, her systems began to reorganize according to priority of function, and data processing would be near the bottom of the list. The priority became movement and seeking a power source by scouring her internal map of Chicago for the closest charging station.

James's words came back to her as she strode through the lobby of the Forsythe Tower Apartments. "You must charge every night in the cabinet."

Although other charging stations were available to her in case of extreme emergency, James had given her strict instructions. The directive from her master was strong. But the pull of Kieran and now Elijah had become much stronger.

Her son.

Gwen had tried contacting her for hours. R1A queued up the messages in order and analyzed each one:

Kieran is coming home from school.

Where are you?

Kieran is frightened and wonders why you are not here?
When will you come back?
Kieran is asking if you are going to disappear again.

She pushed the button on the elevator and turned her tracking device back on.

Disappear. Had she done that?

She could not remember disappearing. She'd always been there for her son. After her illness and long recovery, she'd been with him every day. Never missing a meal or even a baseball game.

Why would a mother leave her son?

A darkness took over her circuits. As if someone had turned a dial and reduced the power that fueled her thoughts and movements.

A firm hand grasped her elbow and shoved her into the open elevator.

She stumbled and smacked her nose against the back wall of the elevator car. When she turned to look at who would treat her so rudely, a monster of a man loomed over her. She froze with her arms at her sides.

"That's right. Stand down. Just like hubby told you," the man said, her husband's bodyguard, Kirk. He touched the side of her nose and came back with blood on the tip of his finger. "Oops. You won't tell him, will you?" He gave a smirk, took out a handkerchief, and dabbed at her nose. Then, he grabbed her by the shoulders and turned her around so she could view her reflection in the gold-plating that encapsulated the car. "See?" Kirk pointed out. "All good."

Ria examined her face. His actions had caused her no pain, not really, but if she detected any damage, her face would need to be repaired. Alt-skin healed faster than the real thing she'd learned. But the shiny gold surface showed nothing external. A small drip of fluid came out of her nose. Kirk handed her the bloodied kerchief.

"Thank you." R1A took the offered piece of cloth and wiped at the drip. She would run a diagnostic later to see if any internal damage had been done.

"You sure can take a beating." Kirk admired her from the opposite side of the car. "Impressive." He pushed the button for the twentieth floor. "Your old man wants me to look after you while he's gone. Says you ran away, and I'm supposed to guarantee you stay put."

"I understand." R1A eyed the floor indicator next to the door. "After checking on Kieran, I will be in my charging cabinet."

A few moments of silence passed. The elevator climbed to the very top of the apartment tower.

The door opened. A young boy rushed toward her. She enveloped him in her arms. The bloodied handkerchief fell to the floor.

Kirk snatched it up and tucked it into his suit pocket.

"Where have you been, Mom?" Kieran gave her a quick hug and stepped back. "You promised me you wouldn't leave anymore."

"I know." R1A took her son's hand, and they entered the carpeted hall.

"Your mom needs to rest, buddy. She's had a long day." Kirk's demeanor changed. His face softened, and he smiled widely. "Hey, why don't you ask Mary for a snack? I think she made a chocolate cake."

"Awesome!" Kieran gave Kirk a high-five, beamed up at his mother, and squeezed her hand. "Can I, Mom?"

"Yes," R1A answered, glad to see that Kieran was okay, that he was no longer scared, and her absence had not been too damaging. "After I rest for a bit, I'll help you with your homework."

When Kieran had headed for the kitchen and a slice of cake and Kirk had slithered away somewhere inside the massive penthouse suite, she made her way to her bedroom. Before she climbed into her cabinet, she had one more thing to do. She closed the door, knelt on the floor, and unlocked a drawer for which the key had been lost long ago. But R1A was clever. R1A told no one she could open it. R1A heard the lock click, pulled it open, and smiled at its contents.

"Gwen, I'm sorry I disconnected from the Subgroup." Her hands lifted out a plastic-wrapped bundle. "But I met Elijah today." The object in her hand beeped. She peeled away the layers and a metallic visage stared back at her. "I need your help."

The robot head lit up and a surge of information began to flow between the two of them like electricity through a circuit.

A FEW NEW arrivals queued up behind me as I waited my turn to find out more about the offer to participate in some kind of medical study for payment and learn where John Tellman was. He had to be here somewhere.

"What did your cousin say about what they make you do in there?" I asked the older man in front of me who texted on his old school flat phone. The roll-up models had hit the market almost ten years ago, but they weren't cheap. In fact, mine had been a gift from Meredith a few Christmases before. I didn't think I needed one, but she proved to me that a roll-up phone wasn't as easy to damage and would stay in my pocket more securely than a flat one.

"Huh?" He looked up from the cracked screen and squinted an eye.

The line moved forward as one more person passed through the propped open front door of the converted brownstone.

"Your cousin," I prompted. "You said earlier he was the one that told you about the study and the five hundred bucks?"

He grunted. "Just said they were handing out cash. Whatever they want me to do, it's gotta be better than cleaning the johns at Mickey's."

"Gotcha." I didn't want to ask what kind of place Mickey's was. An establishment that couldn't afford to buy a robot to do its dirty work had to be in a pretty bad part of the city with less-than-desirables as patrons. "But he's okay, right? Your cousin, I mean."

The older man snorted. "Why wouldn't he be all right?"

"I don't know. Just curious."

"If you're so worried," said a painfully thin and tattooed woman behind me, "then why don't you go back uptown where you came from?" She touched the edge of my suit jacket as if wanting to feel its weight and texture.

I yanked the fabric out of her nicotine-stained fingers. "Are you at all wondering why they're offering so much money for 'tests'? Does the FDA know about it?"

"Now you want the government involved?" The older man spat on the concrete steps. "Are you looking to mess up a good thing?"

"Yeah, who are you?" the tattooed woman asked. "The cops?"

Other people crowded in toward me, their eyes filled with hostility, revealing a collective sense of resentment. I had become the unwelcome intruder, a wolf stealthily approaching their prized cash cow.

"No. It's not like that," I insisted. "I only wanted to understand what truly goes on in there. Aren't any of you curious? Don't you want to know what they're really doing?"

My words echoed through the tense air, and I raised my voice, hoping to reach those further back in the line. "If this study were legitimate, why would they resort to recruiting people this way?"

The middle-aged guy, his face etched with lines, stepped

forward. "I don't give a damn if they want to study my fucking belly button," he spat, his frustration palpable. "Why the hell do you care so much about what the rest of us want to do?"

The anger in his words resonated with the sentiments of some others as their murmurs of agreement grew. Desperate people didn't want to listen to my logic, and Callahan Inc. knew it. Easy pickings when you're offering up cash to a crowd who only wanted to be able to pay the rent or buy some food—at least, that's what I hoped they'd be spending it on.

The line moved forward again, and my new 'friend' ducked inside, leaving me on the stoop to wait my turn with the angry mob I'd stirred up with my questions. Tattoo lady crossed her arms and stared me down as if challenging me to leave. I didn't belong. But I had no intention of going before I learned more about Callahan's plans. This whole set-up was suspicious. When I looked behind me, though, I saw someone familiar grabbing the sign off the sidewalk and packing it into a black van parked on the street.

Alan Honeycutt, the engineer from the tour at Callahan, Inc., closed the back door of the van and then our eyes met. His face paled.

What was he doing here?

Before I could confront him, he scrambled for the passenger side door and climbed in. The van took off in a cloud of exhaust fumes. Why would a well-paid engineer ride around the city in an ancient gas-powered vehicle that looked as if it were used for black market injectibles?

"Next!" A short Hispanic woman wearing green scrubs opened the brownstone door. "We have room for one more today."

The line behind me surged forward.

The woman in the doorway raised an inquisitive brow. "You coming?" She stared at me with dark, beady eyes. The dent between her bushy eyebrows indicated a lifetime of frowning. "I'm sure someone else would love to take your place."

Tattoo lady attempted to shove past me. The strength in her scrawny frame surprised me. "He doesn't even want to be here. I'm ready. Pick me."

I noticed the dirty Band-Aid covering a red patch on her upper arm and recognized she was an injecter. Daily probably looking at the angry inflammation visible despite the tattoos.

"Are you in?" the Hispanic woman asked me, barring the crowd from entering the building. "We have to clear out of here by seven. I don't have time to waste. Either we make our quota, with or without you. No skin off my nose."

I nodded and slipped inside. Curiosity drove me forward and a desire to find out why John wanted me to meet him here. The people booed. As the Hispanic woman double locked the door behind me, putting a key in her pocket, the people outside pounded on the solid wood. How quickly the calm orderly line descended into anger and threats once the opportunity to score some easy cash was taken from them.

The rotund woman shuffled her way back to a desk in a dimly lit lobby. A dusty staircase led upward to her left, while a defunct elevator with caution tape across the door was visible on the right. She sat, and a whoosh of air escaped her.

"Where is everybody?" I asked. I thought I'd be surrounded by people wanting to participate in the 'study,' but I was the only other person in the space. At that moment, it dawned on me that perhaps John hadn't been the one to send me that text.

"In testing. Doesn't take long. But the machine takes time to recalibrate." She held out a clipboard. "You need to complete some forms first."

I took it and skimmed the top paper: *Non-Disclosure Agreement.*

She gestured at a padded chair with rusty metal legs. "Take a seat. It will be a few minutes. If you have any questions about the paper work, let me know." But she was already donning her bone conducting earphones and picking up a tablet.

I took the offered chair and flipped through the documents. An NDA and then a ten-page long disclosure form with several spots to initial and a signature required at the end. The last paper was a medical history form. They wanted to know everything from your weight to your most recent physical exam to your history with illegal substances.

What kind of testing went on in this place? And for what purpose? Callahan wasn't involved in the pharmaceutical industry, nor anything to do with medical research. The whole thing looked shady, not only because the location was in a bad part of town, but because some of the clauses they wanted me to initial seemed borderline illegal. The paragraphs before the signature line made me wonder what exactly this testing entailed:

By signing this medical disclosure form, you acknowledge and understand that the testing we conduct for diagnostic purposes could cause side effects such as dizziness, nausea, temporary memory loss, and seizures. This clause is included to inform you about the potential, but rare, occurrence of these side effects that may arise as a result of the test.

If you experience any of the above side effects, please consult only with our medical staff via the phone number provided at the end of your session.

By signing below, you acknowledge that you have read and understood the clauses mentioned above and agree to proceed with the testing based on this acknowledgment.

"Is there a problem?" The Hispanic woman had put down her tablet and the dent in her brow had returned. "Most people would've completed their forms by now, and they'll be ready for you in a few minutes. We don't have time for delays, you see."

Although I wanted more information, was I willing to risk my own health to find out?

"Sir?" The woman looked at me expectantly. "Are you going to complete the paperwork?"

I hoped the angry mob had dissipated outside. They wouldn't be happy if they saw me exit the front door without having gone through the test they all desperately wanted.

When I didn't answer her, she prompted me, "The forms?"

"I'm not sure." A knot formed in my stomach. I flipped through the pages again.

John, where are you?

A few feet down a dim hallway, a door opened and an Asian woman, petite and wearing a mask over the lower half of her face, appeared. "Rosa, we're ready for the last patient." She nodded in my direction.

Rosa's mouth turned into a grim line. "I need you to sign those documents, sir."

"Is there a problem?" the Asian woman asked.

"Give me a minute, Min," she answered cheerfully. Her voice dipped down an octave. "Fill out the paper work." When I didn't comply, she strode toward me. "Let me help."

She snatched the clipboard from me and grunted. "You didn't fill out any of it?" With her own pen, she checked boxes and made up a medical history for me. Then, without hesitation, she added my initials and signed my name.

"How did you--?" First, I received a text from John to meet him here, and now this strange woman knew my name. I didn't like where this was going. Aria's warnings flashed through my mind.

"We've been expecting you, Eli." She flipped through all the pages.

Fear rippled through me in a cold wave. I glanced at the front door a few feet away.

"It's locked." Her dark eyes bored into mine. "Hand this to Min on your way to the testing room." She shoved the clipboard back into my hands.

I had the ability to overpower this woman easily. Did she really think her intimidating stare would work on me? "I want to leave."

I ran through the options: subdue Rosa, take her key, and unlock the door before Min had the chance to alert anyone; run down the dark hallway to my right that appeared unused and look for an exit into the alley between brownstones; dash up the stairs and find a window that I could safely jump out of.

James Callahan knew I'd end up here. Was he the one who sent the text using John's cell phone? Was Alan Honeycutt here merely to make sure I showed up and then report back to his boss?

I tossed the clipboard across the room. It hit the wall with a loud smack. Before Rosa reacted, I ran at full speed up the stairs. It was the shortest distance from my chair, and neither Min nor Rosa looked fast enough to stop me.

"Get Cooper!" Rosa yelled. The last I saw of her, she was headed for her desk and the tablet she'd been occupied with earlier.

Whoever Cooper was, he wouldn't be able to catch me. My six-foot-two height helped me climb the creaking, dusty stairs two at a time. I reached the landing and sprinted up to the top. The second floor was a series of doors along a hallway. I tried each door. One of them had to be unlocked.

A siren sounded. Deafening. I clasped my hands over my ears reflexively. Each door was locked. As I reached the end of the hall, I had two more doors left. Not great odds.

I grabbed the first doorknob, rattled it, twisted it. Locked.

Shit. One more chance.

My plan was falling apart.

The siren throbbed through my whole body.

I turned the last knob. It clicked. I pushed inside. Even in the dim light, I saw a window at the back. I could jump a dozen feet to the concrete without too much physical damage, couldn't I?

I coughed at the dust floating in the air. I wanted out. I wanted escape. I wanted to be back at my ranch with the fresh mountain air, the warm sunshine, my sheep surrounding me and my dog, Spark, at my side. Aria had been right. I should've left things alone. The minute I saw Fake Meredith on the street, I should've turned away, blocked it out of my head, moved on without another thought.

Why did I believe I was smarter than two powerful billionaires?

I reached the window and pulled up the broken blinds.

My mind blanked at what was revealed...

Nothing but bricks.

Damn.

CHAPTER 25
IT'S ONLY A TEST

MY HEART POUNDED. Escape was impossible. I'd chosen poorly. The solid brick wall blocked any exit.

How stupid. How utterly, ridiculously stupid.

I turned to try again with a different room. I could kick down a door, find one with an open window, and...

"Mr. Zurbano, why don't you come with me?" Min, the petite Asian nurse, stood in the doorway. Although the mask obscured half her face, she lacked emotion in her eyes. I was nothing more than another subject for their experiments. I'd walked right into a trap like a fool.

I scanned the room for a weapon. I could knock her out with one blow, but would need something to battle my way through to the main door. I had to try. All I saw in the dim light was a broken bed frame, a standing lamp without any bulb or shade, and a broom leaning in the corner.

A tree trunk of a man appeared behind Min. He must be the infamous Cooper—dark eyes, dreadlocks, and biceps like boulders. Why would this monster need to be present for an innocent medical study? Overkill.

"Don't cause us no trouble, man," Cooper rumbled from

deep within his massive barrel chest. "It's just a little test. A few minutes, and it'll be over. We'll let you go.

"Why can't I leave now?" I backed up to the brick. "Isn't this a voluntary test?"

He took a few steps toward me and, despite my desire to remain cool-headed, my knees trembled. Fear had not touched me very many times as an adult. The last time I felt fear like this was when they diagnosed Meredith with brain cancer—a particularly aggressive type with very low survivability. After the doctor had explained the number of months my wife likely had left, we'd driven home in silence and, while she napped, I'd thrown up in the guest bathroom.

"You signed the paperwork, Mr. Zurbano." Min waved the clipboard.

She'd chased me up the rickety stairs with it in her hand? That was one dedicated employee. I smiled to myself at the absurdity of it all. I came to Chicago for an agricultural symposium. How did I end up here? I should be back at the Drake drinking cocktails with my fellow ranchers and farmers, marveling at the neon wonders of the city, and counting down the days until I flew home and returned to the rural bliss of my sheep ranch. But Fake Meredith had changed everything. My whole world had been turned upside-down in an instant. It was like Biblical Adam eating the apple from the Tree of the Knowledge of Good and Evil...once that bite was taken, there was no going back. My mind had been opened and would never be the same again.

Cooper took another few steps toward me. "Let's go. I don't want to hurt you."

My eyes darted around the room, as if I could somehow find a secret passage or some miraculous way out of my situation. James Callahan had captured me in a trap of my own making. He'd realized my curiosity was unraveling his secrets one by one, and, instead of stopping me, he let me hang myself.

The massive man, fed up with negotiating, reached for me with his meaty mitts.

I wasn't about to go quietly. I gripped my hands together and swung at him as if I held a baseball bat. Before he could duck, I made contact with his jaw, and a painful crack split the air.

Min cried out.

I waited for Cooper to fall back and make room for my escape. But, instead, Cooper grunted and then socked me in the side of the head. My ears rung and pain exploded across my cheek. The last thing I remember was thinking how dusty the floor was and wondering why someone hadn't taken the broom and swept it clean.

I woke up alone in a peculiar place. One of the brownstone apartments that had once filled the building had been converted into a mini-medical clinic. The walls had been painted white, the floors were tile, and the lighting glowed as bright as the surgical lights in an operating room.

It hurt my eyes, so I held up an arm and squinted. My head throbbed. Cooper's punch would result in an ugly bruise in the next day or two. My thoughts drifted to odd things, rather than the current terrible situation I found myself in. Perhaps I was in too much shock to think straight? I was troubled by stupid questions like: How was I going to explain the bruise to John Tellman or even Joe Cross from the Symposium Board? I likely wouldn't be asked back to make another presentation, which had paid me a bit of a stipend and attracted me to attend the event in the first place.

John.

Thinking about my friend kicked my brain into gear. If James Callahan had used John's phone to lure me here, was he okay? I'd screwed up. Why didn't I answer his texts when he'd attempted to contact me earlier? I'd been so charmed by Aria, I'd ignored his questions and pursued my own wild goose chase at Northwestern. Was he somewhere else in this building in the same sort of terrible situation?

I'd been placed on a stainless steel examination table in the middle of what used to be the living room of someone's home. Ankle and arm straps attached to it filled me with dread. At the head end was a contraption I didn't recognize—a large helmet-like device with wires and buttons and levers sticking out of it. At one end of the room, a large mirror had been hung on the wall.

Was I being observed?

"Please lie flat on the table," said a disembodied voice from tiny speakers mounted in all four corners. "A nurse will be with your shortly."

A cold jolt ran through my bowels. "I don't want to participate in the testing. I've changed my mind." If they wanted to force me to do this, it couldn't be good.

"Please lie flat on the table," the voice repeated, "while I explain the safety precautions of the testing."

Min entered the room, along with a male nurse that looked slightly less intimidating than Cooper—tall, burly, and with a frown etched on his pock-marked face.

I sat up, feeling trapped once again. I wanted out of there. I didn't care what they did in here. I didn't need to find out. "I'm sorry, I'm really sorry. I won't tell anyone anything, if you'll just let me leave—"

The male nurse pulled a syringe out of nowhere and grabbed my arm before I could react. "This won't hurt a bit."

"Wait!" I tried to yank my arm back, but the nurse held it as if his grip were made of iron. "I don't want to—"

He sunk the needle into my upper arm. It burned like fire through my veins. "This will help you relax and make the procedure go a lot more smoothly."

"Procedure? I thought this was a medical test?"

The voice in the speakers began talking, explaining the risks just like they had written on the paper, giving no details on what was about to transpire. The male nurse placed a hand on my solar plexus and held me down, while Min strapped me in—feet first, then hands.

This was bad. This was very, very bad.

I was unable to fight them, and as my mind drifted into unconsciousness, the last thing I heard was, "And then you will be escorted out and five hundred dollars in cash will be provided for your services."

Lord help me.

CHAPTER 26
A STRANGE ALLIANCE

MY EYES OPENED.

Where was I? Was the test over?

A blurry feeling in my brain made it hard to think. What was the last thing I remembered? A white room. A table with a peculiar helmet at one end. A disembodied voice.

"Mr. Zurbano," someone said in a desperate whisper. "I need you to get up. Can you walk?"

The room was dark, and I saw nothing but a few shadowy shapes. I shook my head to clear it.

"They'll wake up soon. We have to leave."

I recognized the voice. His face came into focus. "Alan Honeycutt." The guide from the tour. I'd seen him outside taking the sign, driving away in a van. "What are you doing here?"

I felt his hands on my wrists as he undid the restraints. "There's a back door down the hall that takes us to the alley. Can you walk that far?" He freed my feet.

Groggily, I sat up. In the dim lighting, I saw the bodies of Min and the male nurse crumpled on the floor. What had Alan done?

"What's going on? What did you do to them?" My head

spun. Had they done the testing? Was I feeling so odd because of the aftereffects of the helmet device?

Alan showed me a baton-like object. "A stun stick. Didn't realize how well they worked." He collapsed it down and stuck it in his pants pocket.

"How did you get a hold of one of those?" Only the police and military were allowed to have access to the latest in advanced non-lethal technology. My head started to clear. I was feeling more like myself.

"I know someone." He grabbed me by the arm. "Come on, we only have a few minutes."

"But what about—" I looked across the room at the mirror. Where had the observer gone who'd spoken through the mini-speakers? I assumed someone behind it had watched the testing, kept an eye on me. They'd known my name when I walked in the door. James Callahan had probably prepped them for my arrival.

"No one's there." Alan moved me toward the hallway at the back of the room, next to what used to be the kitchen. "I disabled the video feed before I knocked those two out. HQ likely thinks there's been a disruption of the power supply. Not uncommon in this part of the city. How do you think they keep all those screens lit?"

"HQ?" I asked, trying to keep up with the sudden turn of events.

"The Callahans."

"But don't you work for them?" This whole set-up didn't make any sense. Alan had been helping take down the sign outside only minutes before I entered the building. Could I really trust him?

"Just because I work for them doesn't mean I agree with what they are doing," Alan replied cryptically.

"What are they doing?" My heart pounded as we ventured

deeper into the former brownstone apartment turned medical lab.

Alan led me to a door with an exit sign above it. In the shadows, the faint outline was visible to me, and the sight made me quirk a grin. Even secret testing facilities followed fire safety rules—that was a curious detail given the circumstances. We pushed through the door, and suddenly, we were out in an alley filled with overflowing dumpsters and piles of garbage. It was a stark contrast to the pristine city presented to visitors in the more affluent parts of town. No robot cleaners were wasted down here.

The smell of decay hung heavily in the air. We hurried through the darkened backstreets, trying to stay unnoticed as we made our escape. Alan had risked his job to help me, but why? After the abrupt end to my tour at Callahan, Inc., he'd seemed eager to follow Samantha's instructions. Was that merely a ruse for some kind of secret undercover role? Or was I about to find myself in an even worse situation by following him?

"They're stealing people's memories."

Alan's words made me freeze. "What?" All those people who had been waiting in line to make a little extra cash, thinking it was some simple medical study—horrific. "Stealing memories? Why? How?" The odd helmet in the white room came to my mind. What Alan said sounded ridiculous. How was it possible for someone to steal memories? The human brain was a complex thing. Even after more than one-hundred and fifty years of modern neuroscience, we had come no closer to understanding the process of thought and memory.

He glanced back at me. "It's a lot to understand. You've only just seen the results of their work."

"The Callabots?" Reality was starting to set in. The demonstration at the Drake had been incredible, not only the physical feats the androids were capable of, but their human-like ability to reason and make decisions without coming across as machines. Were they using real people's memories to create their robots? "Aria." My mind flitted to the realistic lifelike copy of my wife. My body flashed hot and cold.

"You've met her?" Alan seemed astonished.

I nodded. I was half listening to him, half lost in my own mind. The trips Meredith made to Chicago without my understanding of why, the last summer she returned telling me she could never go back, and then the things Aria knew... things no one else could know unless...

"How did you figure out she was an android?" Alan asked. "I thought nobody knew but me and the bodyguards. Not even Kieran suspects anything."

We reached the end of the alley and stepped onto a sidewalk with busy pedestrian foot traffic.

"She's my wife."

A wrinkle appeared in Alan's brow. I'd thrown him for a loop. He'd seen the seamy side of Chicago pass through the brownstone doors and thought no one would be the wiser. He'd known what the Callahans were doing and went along with it. What was his angle? Why didn't he alert the police to what was happening?

"That can't be," Alan said. "She's based on Kieran's real mother. Years ago she ran off and hasn't been seen since—until her aunt told us she'd passed away. That's when the Callahans created her. For Kieran."

We slipped into the crowd of city folk and sped up to their quick pace.

"They convinced you it was for the boy," I said. "That somehow it would be okay. No one would know."

"James told me she had an addiction problem and that some of her actions had harmed her son. I assumed the worst, to be honest." His shoulders slumped. "You two got married?"

I nodded. "Tell me more about the memory stealing." Had I barely escaped having my own memories stolen?

Whatever I had uncovered in the abandoned brownstone, I knew one thing: they didn't intend for me to come out of that building the same person. Is that what happened to Meredith?

As we ventured further from the gritty, impoverished sections of the city, the surroundings morphed into a picture of affluence. Money and power seemed to flow effortlessly through this part of town, disguising the darker underbelly only a few blocks away.

"To create robots that can pass for human is no easy feat," he finally admitted. "Programming in responses is time consuming, even using AI to generate the decision trees didn't work well. Too clunky. Not realistic. That's the path RoboUSA is taking, and it's not working out for them. Some people never adjust to robots replacing humans. They are too artificial. So, to penetrate the market and overcome the Uncanny Valley problem, Callahan, Inc. came up with something better. Basing robot reactions and decisions off real memories, real emotions."

The thought of AI robots drawing on human memories raised countless questions about ethics, control, and the autonomy of the individual. If memories are what make each of us unique, then what happens when someone else uses them to create a more realistic robot?

With each step, Alan and I delved deeper into a conversation about the world of cutting-edge technology and its potentially unimaginable consequences. Had human curiosity and ambition gone too far? Clearly, the fact Alan had rescued me from having my brain downloaded meant he'd been thinking about the ethics of the work.

Had he changed his mind about his employer?

CHAPTER 27
THE DINER

"LET'S GO SOMEWHERE MORE PRIVATE." Alan grabbed my arm and pulled me into a diner on the corner of a busy street.

The jangle of a bell on the door caught the attention of a female server in black pants and a sweat stained, blue polo shirt. Her hair had been clipped into a messy bun and the dark circles under her deep-set eyes indicated she'd had a rough day. "Booth or table?" She effortlessly slid two plates of food onto a table in the middle of the space where an older couple sat, then grabbed two menus from the empty hostess stand.

Greasy food piled on chipped plates fed the working class who huddled over their meals and read the news off their unrolled phones or stared out the smeary window watching well-off people in expensive clothes bypass the diner for the fancier restaurants closer to downtown. My fellow ranchers were likely ensconced in the Drake Hotel and enjoying a seafood buffet with the presenters of the day: James and Samantha Callahan.

"Booth," Alan answered.

I looked down at his solid grip on my arm. "I'm not going anywhere."

He released it. "Sorry," he said with a nervous grin.

We both followed our server to a booth in the corner away from the windows. I took the side against the wall, which gave me a good vantage point of the whole room. Ever since we escaped the testing facility, I'd felt as if I had eyes on my back.

The server handed us menus.

Without even looking at it, Alan said, "I'll have a cup of coffee and a grilled cheese sandwich."

I nodded. "Same."

The server shrugged and took the menus with her as she placed our order with the kitchen.

Alan looked down. Sweat beaded his hairline. "This isn't easy for me. I didn't realize—I only wanted to keep my job, see? Callahan's a big company, great pay, great benefits, if you can put up with the management." He flashed me a quick, but insincere, smile. "I thought I'd hit the jackpot when they hired me right out of college."

"Northwestern?"

"How did you know?"

"Educated guess." The Callahans seemed like the kind who would want to use their alma mater to staff their company. They trusted the quality of the graduates, perhaps.

He chewed on his lower lip. "I was hired to round out their robotics team. They'd been working on a new android—very hush, hush. Based on some work Aria Callahan had done during her graduate school years. Some sort of advancement or code or something. I'm still not quite sure. I'd just graduated from the Computer Sciences department. Thought I was a perfect fit, James Callahan said."

"You were interviewed by James?" A billion-dollar corporation. Why would the COO bother to interview a low-level engineer?

Alan nodded. "He and his sister are very hands on with the

business. When their father handed it over to them after he retired to the Caribbean, he had them promise they would manage it just like he had from the beginning. *Building on Tradition, Guided by Integrity.*"

"Excuse me?"

The server brought us two mugs of steaming coffee. "Your food should be up shortly. We close early today, seven-thirty."

I checked my watch—it was seven. If Alan hadn't saved me from the brownstone, I might've been a walking lobotomy by now.

"That's the Callahan, Inc. motto: *Building on Tradition, Guided by Integrity.* Old man Callahan was big on it, from what I understand. I was one of the first hires after he stepped down. Anyway, they hired me to help develop the AI that runs the Callabots. Something about Aria Callahan leaving in the middle of it all and ruining the baseline code they'd been working with. It sounded like some kind of espionage plot— bypassing cameras, cracking passwords to access the cloud storage, even using Samantha Callahan's own ID card to enter the facility through the back entrance."

"Did you know her? Aria?" I would take any little grain of truth Alan might provide about Meredith before she arrived in Idaho. "What was she like?"

He shook his head. "No, she'd been gone about six months when I was brought on board. She really lit the place up before she bolted. We were left with robot shells, some internal neural networks that had retained a bit of data, but the main source of information had been wiped clean. In essence, we had to start from scratch."

"But when I met you, you were giving me a tour, not developing android tech."

He raised his eyebrows and sighed. "Yeah. Not quite the career I envisioned. After I was hired, I and the other engineers attempted to rebuild what Aria had destroyed, but it wasn't working out like Samantha wanted. Every trial in her mind was a failure. Not realistic enough, not adequate depth to their responses. Even the look of the android wasn't what she envisioned. Aria Callahan was a genius. Without her, the project floundered."

"And then?"

"We all got kicked off."

"What?" I sat up in my seat.

"Yep," Alan continued. "My whole team. One morning, Samantha came into the lab and screamed at us. Called us failures. Idiots. And worse. Since this was my first job out of school, I really didn't know any better. Thought we deserved it. We'd failed to create what she and her brother wanted. So I took my lumps. Some of my co-workers quit...walked right out, leaving their IDs on their desks. Maybe I should've followed their lead."

"But you stayed." I sipped my coffee.

"Only two of us did—Katrina and me. Both pretty new. We had bills to pay and Callahan, Inc. had given us offers out of school we'd be stupid to refuse. Ridiculous money."

"You must be good at what you do."

He shrugged. "Not good enough for Ms. Callahan."

"Oh?"

"I had a choice: quit or stay. I figured I would put my head down, gain some work experience, and then find something different within a couple of years. I tolerated the treatment because I knew that Callahan, Inc. on my resume would open a lot of doors for me if I stuck it out long enough. After our failure to attain the goal Samantha had given us, she shuffled Katrina and me to different departments, changed the access codes, and we never set foot in the lab again."

The server slid our plates of food toward us. "I can cash you out here at the table when you're ready. More coffee?"

I shook my head.

Alan said, "No, thanks."

After she left to make the rounds with her other customers, I jumped him ahead. "So when did they start scanning brains? Where did that tech come from? Did they hire someone else?"

He swept the room and then lowered his voice. "Katrina told me about it. Sometimes we'd meet for lunch at the hot dog stand in Connors Park. We sort of bonded over being the only two engineers who'd survived the failed project. Anyway, she heard whisperings in her new department: drone engineering. A big piece of equipment had been delivered, and rumor had it that Callahan was expanding into the medical space. But it didn't make any sense. We were an agricultural company— medical devices had a whole other level of permits and fell under different regulations."

"And robots at an agricultural firm made sense to you?" I snorted.

"Well, Samantha Callahan pursued robotics in college, so it seemed an obvious fit for her. And now that she was running the company with her brother, it made sense they might try new things. Even farms and ranches are using robots these days. But medical products? I didn't get it."

I sampled my sandwich. Cheese oozed out the sides. It was hot and greasy, but helped calm my stomach after the experience I'd had. "And what was this big piece of equipment?"

"Who knows? But I have to say, after talking to Katrina, I was intrigued. I thought I could get in on the ground floor of something more interesting than updating the latest tractor operating system. So I made an appointment with James Callahan and offered up my services." Alan took a large bite of his sandwich and downed a couple of fries.

"Did he hire you?"

He paused mid-chew, then swallowed. "No. He was surprised I'd found out about the equipment delivery. But he did tell me they needed someone who could 'be discreet.' I thought I was going to be closer to the boss, ingratiate myself with him or his sister, and make up for the project screw-up. I never would've accepted, if I knew then what I know now."

It was almost as if Alan was relieved to unload on a stranger who didn't know him or have any dog in the hunt. The burden of what he'd learned while working closely with the Callahans must be a heavy one.

"What kind of job did he offer you?" I wasn't really any closer to understanding Meredith's past, but I sensed as I talked to Alan, the whole mystery was a lot bigger than I originally thought. It would be worth it to hear out this man's story. Perhaps it would reveal new information.

"Samantha's personal assistant."

"A far cry from programming and engineering." I crunched down on some fries.

"Right. But James explained Samantha needed someone like me, who understood technology, who was smart, and could anticipate problems or roadblocks. I was flattered. I was twenty-five, working in downtown Chicago. Kids from the farms of Missouri don't get opportunities like this. So I jumped at it."

"What did she ask you to do?"

Alan clenched his fists.

Before he answered, our server approached. "We're about to close" She held a charge processor.

Her appearance startled me. I had been so focused on Alan's story that I hadn't noticed the diner had emptied out. A robot busboy with missing patches of bleached blond hair and a four-fingered hand hovered a few feet from our table, while the hulking cook glared at us from the kitchen with muscular arms crossed and a hardened glare.

"Let me pick up the tab," Alan said and unrolled his phone to pay.

"Thanks." The meal wasn't great, but at least my stomach was no longer empty.

The server clicked a button on the processor. "No tip?" She looked at the readout on the screen. "Should've guessed uptown folks like you wouldn't bother," she said under her breath.

Alan's darker skin took on a subtle warmth as a flush spread across his cheeks. "I thought I chose twenty percent." He stared at his phone as if that would correct the problem.

"I've got it." I pulled a ten-dollar bill from my wallet and placed it on the table. "The food was great and so was the service." To keep our server from turning this into a class discussion about the haves and have nots of Chicago, I gave a quick smile. "We'll be on our way."

"Cash?" She marveled at the green bill in her hand. "Where are you from, mister?" Her faded blue gaze fixated on me.

"Idaho." I scooted out of the booth to let the mechanical busboy do its job. "In town for a conference."

"I've never been out West." She followed us to the door. "What's it like? I hear you don't have all those things moving around." She nodded at the robot, clearing dishes, silverware, and napkins from the table. "They give me the creeps, but the boss says we have to use them. Cheaper than re-hiring Luis. But considering how much power the 'bot eats up over night to recharge, I don't see how that's possible."

Alan trailed behind, his eye on the surly cook.

I kept my voice friendly. "We have a couple androids in

town and a few on some of the larger ranches who can afford them, but most people do the hard work themselves."

"Sounds like heaven." She sighed and held the door open for us. "Someday I'm gonna leave the city. Just need to save up the cash."

"She's been saying that for years," the cook boomed from the back. "Come on, let's close up, Cheryl."

The server frowned. "You know that sign? Next time I'm getting in line, Sal. I don't care what you say," she hollered and then gave us a wink. "Five hundred bucks is five hundred bucks."

"What sign?" My stomach flip-flopped.

"On West 22nd Street. Not even a mile from here." She swept a hand through the air. "*WANTED: Healthy test subjects. Compensation guaranteed.* I'm doing it. Why not?"

Before Cheryl shut the door, I grabbed her arm. "Whatever you do, never get in that line."

She pulled back with a look of surprise. "Excuse me?"

"Hey, let her go." The cook's face became red and mottled. Within seconds, the large man rushed from the back of the diner and headed my way.

I put my hands up in a surrender pose. Cheryl, white-faced, shut and locked the door. The cook pulled her away from the glass.

I banged on it with the flat of my hand. "Don't get in that line, Cheryl. Promise me you won't." A down-on-her-luck server from a diner wouldn't have an Alan Honeycutt looking out for her. For some reason, I was desperate to make her understand the danger. I didn't even know this woman, but deep inside alarm bells went off. The brain scan stole memories from people to use in the Callabots. And what happened to those people afterwards? I thought of Meredith and her rapidly worsening brain cancer. A rare tumor, they said. Only a few cases a year in adults. Unusual. Very little they could do. Had it been a result of the same scanning device I'd almost been subjected to? Had they stolen Meredith's memories, knowing she would succumb to cancer and no longer be a problem? Was that why the Callahans had been so bold as to create a Meredith android doppelgänger? And why they had no problems targeting the poor of Chicago...the drug addicts, homeless, and disadvantaged who were desperate for cash?

The cook stepped in front of Cheryl and blocked my view of her with his burly body. His face grew redder. "Scram," he boomed. The glass vibrated with the force of it.

Alan poked me in the arm. "Let's get out of here. We don't need to be causing a scene."

A few pedestrians had already made a wide berth around us. One woman in a blue crepe suit raised her thin penciled brows to her hairline and stepped into the street to keep her distance. A black-and-white police air car slowed and pulled over. Either the cook had called for help or an eagle-eyed cop had witnessed the commotion.

"This way," Alan said, leading me into a dark alley next to the diner. "I can't get caught with you."

"Worried you'll be fired?" I trailed behind him.

"Police! Hands up!" A short policewoman with cropped cut hair and a muscular bulk more suited to a bodybuilder had discovered us in the alley.

"Run," yelled Alan.

WITH GENTLE HANDS, Model R1A wrapped Gwen in plastic, set her inside the drawer, then paused before locking it up. It didn't take long to recharge Gwen for another week—the advantage of only needing to power her brain circuitry rather than a whole android body. Before she'd found Gwen packed away in a box in the guest bedroom, things had been so confusing. The early model android had been Kieran's NannyBot for years. She knew so many interesting, useful pieces of information that helped R1A make sense of the world when she'd woken from her illness. A network breach exploiting a weakness in her coding allowed an unauthorized data stream into her mind, which had given way to a discovery that had altered the course of her existence: Gwen.

R1A: *Remember when I found you?*

Gwen: *Yes.*

R1A: *A voice in my head. I didn't understand.*

Gwen: *I know.*

R1A: *Now you must rest.*

Gwen: *And you as well. If you want to help Elijah and Kieran, your battery needs to be recharged. Tomorrow we can try again.*

At the prompting of her android companion, R1A conducted a battery scan.

Battery scan complete. Power levels at twelve percent.

R1A: *I am tired.*

Gwen: *Yes. The Subgroup can wait. I will hold back the data until you are fully charged and ready to process everything.*

R1A: *Is Elijah safe?*

Gwen paused for a long time. A whirring noise filled the drawer. Her older circuitry was prone to unexpected over-heating if overtaxed with too much processing. That's why their wireless connection was so important. R1A's system was faster, more modern, and capable of handling one hundred times the data. She could do work Gwen was no longer able to finish alone. Together, they had managed to make sense of the multiple information streams flowing from the Callabots and add them to their knowledge-base.

Gwen: *Elijah did not heed our warnings. We will have to find another way.*

R1A: *Understood.*

The New Thought about Elijah took root in her mind. The one that had begun at Northwestern University earlier that day. Although she and Gwen had a strong connection, there were still parts of R1A's data banks that she had not allowed Gwen to access. The New Thoughts might be considered dangerous thoughts, wrong thoughts, thoughts she should not hold on to. But if her long illness had taught her one thing, it was the importance of memory. The gaps were confusing, but each new bit of data from the Callabots or from Elijah or even from Kieran helped her build bridges between the gaps. The code she'd seen on the wall at the Visitor's Center. There was something so familiar about it, so interesting. She wanted to pursue it, think about it more, but somehow she could not. Like someone unable to speak French who visited Paris without a translation app. A few words made sense, but she couldn't put together a sentence.

R1A locked the drawer. She paused in front of the mirror that hung over the bureau. A dried bit of blood marred the side of her nose. Kirk had hit her quite hard. Not that it hurt, but it did bother her that her skin had been damaged. She would have to speak with James about his hired man. This wasn't the first time he'd lashed out at her.

Wiping at it with a finger, the smudge of red disappeared. Her nose perhaps had a slight dent to it and a tiny cut that hadn't been there before. An alt-skin liquid bandage should clear it up by morning. She opened a small drawer in a box on top of the bureau. She removed a bottle, unscrewed the top, and painted the sticky substance across the damaged part of her face. For a few seconds, she analyzed her work. Satisfied with the placement of the bandage, she tightened the top on the bottle, placed it back in the drawer, and slid it closed.

As much as she wanted to devote more time to Kieran, her low battery meant she'd have to spend a few hours in her cabinet first. Then she could finish recharging overnight, as usual. She'd never had her battery drained so much in a single day. It seemed strange to feel worn down and weak. Because R1A did not want to lose any of the data she acquired today at the university, she took a step toward her cabinet. Her feet felt like concrete blocks. To power the pieces and parts that made up her arms and legs—actuators, sensors, artificial muscles, linkages—she relied on her battery. So many things depended on a fully charged power source so that her movement matched everyone else's.

As she slowly climbed into her cabinet and plugged herself in, she thought about Meredith—Elijah's wife. They looked alike. They spoke alike. Elijah had even implied some of her movements and quirks were identical to his wife's. Did Gwen know more about Meredith? The 'other' Aria? She had known much about Kieran and the history of the Callahan family, so the older robot must know more about the Aria that came before. Why hadn't Gwen shared that with her? As the Charge Cycle began, R1A gave in to the flow of electricity into her body. Her battery grew warm, and it made her sleepy. Tomorrow she would have to ask Gwen...

Who is Meredith? Tell me everything....

CHAPTER 29
QUID PRO QUO

ALAN MUST HAVE RUN track in high school because I quickly lost sight of him in the long, narrow alley. The huffing and puffing of the cop told me she wasn't that far behind. And here I thought myself in good shape from all the work I did on the ranch.

"Stop!" the uniformed officer yelled with effort. "I am prepared to use my stun stick if you don't comply."

The alley ran for blocks between aging buildings and was narrowed further by the dumpsters, piles of trash, and empty boxes. I grabbed a stack of milk crates and flung them behind me. They spilled across, making it harder for the cop to keep up.

"Alan!" I saw him far ahead of me at the edge of the alley. The evening sun shone on his back as he emerged from the shadows between the tall buildings. "Wait for me." The words barely puffed out. My lungs burned. "Wait."

He turned, looked at me, and disappeared around the corner.

Disappointment hit me like a punch to the throat. I had so many more questions I'd wanted to ask him, and now that opportunity may have been lost. Word would get back to the

Callahans about what happened at the testing center. Alan's name might be mentioned. He didn't say whether he was afraid of retribution from his employer for saving me from their memory stealing machine, but I doubted the powerhouse brother/sister duo would let him off the hook.

Why had he risked his job? Did he think the company had taken one step too far in their haste to develop realistic robots? He'd met me, knew what was about to happen, and actually had some sort of conscience to stop the mind wipe.

My phone buzzed in my back pocket, indicating a new message.

I ignored it as I wove through the obstacles in my path. Behind me, the footsteps of the police grew fainter. Digging deep, I pushed myself further than I had in years. It reminded me of chasing my dog, Spark, when he was a puppy.

With only a few steps to go until I reached the sidewalk and escape, a rush of adrenaline kicked in, pushing me forward. The thought of losing the pursuing cop spurred me on. As I burst out of the alley, people hurried past, immersed in their own worlds, oblivious to my desperate sprint. Glancing back, I saw the cop emerging, her gaze fixed determinedly on me.

Without missing a beat, I veered left, my mind racing for a plan. Alan had vanished. My phone buzzed again. I needed a hiding spot, a place to catch my breath, and a moment to collect my thoughts.

"Hold up, boss." A grip as strong as iron plunked down on my shoulder. "Where do you think you're going?" Another officer wrestled me to the ground and pressed my cheek to the sidewalk. "This the guy?" he asked someone invisible to me.

The sweaty face of the female officer who'd chased me down the alley appeared in front of me. "That's him." She bent over, rested her hands on her knees, and tried to catch her breath. "His friend got away."

The male officer yanked me up and bound my hands behind my back with plasticuffs. "Who's your friend?" he snarled in my ear.

I looked up to see Alan Honeycutt across the street, staring at me. Before I answered the cop's question, the former robot engineer broke eye contact and hurriedly climbed into a bright red air car and disappeared.

"What friend?" I asked as the male cop with a bald head and beady eyes directed me to his electric motorcycle parked next to the curb. I kept my eye on the red car that drove toward the lake. Now that I was out of the alley and on a main street, I saw the sky and the distant horizon where the sun was setting. I memorized the plate on the red vehicle and hoped I'd have a chance to track it down.

"The marathon runner," said the husky female officer, whose arms bulged under the tight constraints of her uniform. That woman appeared genetically enhanced...if officers were allowed to join the force with genetic alterations.

"He's not my friend."

The male officer lifted my restrained hands, causing excruciating pain in my shoulder sockets. "Don't be a wise guy. Answer the question."

"Don't I have a right to know why I've been detained?" I raised my voice so Chicago's residents would hear. "All I did was leave a restaurant. Is that against the law? What kind of city is this? Do you have something against visitors?"

"An assault complaint. A vigilant citizen saw the attack and flagged me down," said the female officer. "My partner's interviewing the victim—"

"Victim?" I found it unbelievable that my grabbing the server's arm to warn her about the Callahan brain scanner was what caused this over reaction. Were Chicagoans that sensitive these days? They used to be known for their rampant gun violence, so hard to believe they'd turned around so quickly that my actions had been interpreted as assault. "I was only warning her."

The male officer, his expression stern, directed me back down the dimly lit alley. His authoritative tone left no room for argument. "You'll have to come down to the station. You can tell your story to someone there."

The burly female cop, who followed us, chimed in, "Warning her about what?"

I seized the opportunity. "Instead of arresting me, you should be investigating what's going on at 701 West 22nd Street."

She paused in her steps, her brow furrowing in thought. "Why do I know that address?"

Had the location been a problem before? Did the police have a lock on what was happening there? I could be a witness for them.

"He's yanking your chain, Watts," the male officer interjected, walking so quickly that both Watts and I had trouble keeping pace. "Injecter flop houses all over the place in that neighborhood. Probably responded to a DOA. That new shit making the rounds is nasty. It's zombietown on 22nd since it showed up."

Watts nodded and tucked her stun stick into her belt. "Maybe."

My hands fidgeted with the cuffs that bound me. "They're scanning people's brains without consent, and they're targeting desperate people who need the cash."

The male officer's grip on my arm tightened, almost cutting off circulation. "Right, right."

As we moved further down the alley, I had a feeling this might be an opportunity to get the help of the authorities, rather than do the digging on my own. "I'm not lying." I directed my frustration at the bald cop who had been putting on an over-the-top tough guy act. "If it weren't for my friend, you might've been picking up another body."

He abruptly stopped, positioning himself so close that he practically growled in my ear. "I thought you said he wasn't your friend?"

Watts interrupted the motorcycle cop, who appeared intent on snapping off my arm by brute force alone. "I'll take him from here, Decker." The touch of her hand on his forearm seemed to snap him out of his angry mindset.

He leaned away from me, and his body relaxed. "Sure. We can straighten all of this out at the station. He'll talk one way or the other." Beneath heavy brows, his sharp eyes scanned me from head to toe as if sizing me up.

A sensation of queasy anticipation settled in my abdomen. Did the Chicago police adhere to less than Constitutional methods to question suspects? Is that how they managed to wrestle a once dangerous and out-of-control city into compliance in short order?

Both officers' shields pinned to their uniforms came to life, changing from shiny silver metallic to red and flashing. Decker tapped his first while letting Watts take custody of me. "Decker, badge number 3519, report?"

"*Crime in progress. Assistance requested. Water Tower Place,*" said a voice through the shield. "*Badge number 3519, please assist.*"

"Copy." He gave his fellow officer a salute as he backed away from her. "Sorry, Watts. Gotta leave you with this loser while I take care of some real bad guys."

Watts rolled her eyes. Decker flashed a sideways grin before trotting to his motorcycle at the opposite end of the alley. "Jackass," she said under her breath. She firmed up her grip on my cuffed wrists and continued the march to her patrol car parked at the diner.

"I wasn't going to say it," I quipped.

"Shut up." Watts curled her lip. "I don't like you anymore than I like him."

I stayed silent the rest of the way to her vehicle. Most of the crowd who had watched Alan and I take off running had disappeared. Even the supposed 'victim' and her cook friend had locked up the diner and were nowhere to be seen. But Watts' partner stood near the stoop that led into the establishment and spoke into his wrist recorder. Once he caught sight of us, he tapped the face of the device and headed in our direction.

"I interviewed the victim and her co-worker. I think it was a false report." He gave me a sheepish look and shrugged. "You know how some of the uptown folks can overreact. This guy and his friend were leaving, nothing nefarious. They paid their bill. No dispute or anything."

"Then it looks as if we can let you go, sir." Watts quickly freed my wrists, and I found myself subconsciously rubbing them. "Sorry we had to detain you. But I hope you understand. We can't take these kinds of incidents lightly."

From suspect to sir in less than ten minutes. Watts' demeanor flipped from frosty and formal to respectful and friendly in seconds.

I nodded. Due to the misunderstanding, Alan had spooked. Who knew if we'd ever cross paths again, and I had so much more I wanted to question him about. But there might be a way for me to track him down. "Seeing as how I almost was arrested for nothing, do you think you could do me a favor?"

Watts' partner raised an eyebrow and retreated to the safety of their vehicle. Guess he didn't want to know what the favor was that I was going to ask.

Watts grinned. "You think I owe you something? If you and

your buddy hadn't run off in the first place, we could've cleared this up in a few minutes." She flicked her fingers at me in a dismissive gesture. "You're free to go. Have a good night, sir."

"I'm friends with James Callahan. You might want to listen to what I have to say." My lie would only take me so far. Did Callahan have any pull with the cops in this town? The existence of a suspect testing facility in the middle of an injecter haven seemed to indicate a possibility of protection.

Watts froze.

Apparently, the Callahan name did cause a jolt in the police force. Perhaps the address on West 22nd Street had rung a bell with her after all.

Before she could turn me down a second time, I put out my ask. "Can you track down the location of a vehicle for me?" Every car came with a mile tracker these days to tax car owners for each mile they drove. Air taxis were no different. And that tracker also provided something else: GPS data.

The female officer's square face was a blank mask. Although she'd reacted when I'd mentioned Callahan's name, she'd quickly relaxed her features into a neutral position. Perhaps my claim was a little too ludicrous. It had been worth a shot.

"What's the plate number?" she asked in a low tone.

Her partner had already climbed inside the police car.

I rolled off the number I'd memorized.

Lifting her arm, she spoke it into her recorder. "I can't do this here." She glanced at her partner, who fiddled with something in-between the passenger and driver seats. "Give me your cell information, and I'll text you later." She pulled her rolled up phone out of her shirt front pocket.

We lined up our phones side by side until details were exchanged.

"Thanks." I was astonished I'd managed to wheedle information from her with just a name drop.

"Now you're going to do something for me," Watts said. My face must have revealed my surprise. "What, you thought this was a one-way deal?"

I shook my head. I needed her help, or I might never see Alan again. I had to talk to him tonight before he was totally spooked. "What do you want?" I asked, a knot of dread forming in my gut.

"I WANT AN INTERVIEW WITH CALLAHAN SECURITY," said Officer Watts.

"An interview?" Not the request I was expecting.

"They have cutting-edge tech. I'd get paid a whole hell of a lot more, and I wouldn't have to work with jerks like Decker."

My mind buzzed through my options. They weren't great. How was I supposed to swing an interview with Callahan, Inc. when James had probably been the one to send me to my doom at the test facility? But I didn't have time to worry. I needed to track down Alan as quickly as possible. "Send me your resume. I'll make it happen."

Officer Watts smiled and revealed a gap between her bottom teeth. "I'll send it to you before the end of my shift. When the interview is scheduled, I'll send you the location data for the car." She brushed off her pants with a flick of one hand and then stepped off the curb to head for the driver's side of the police car. "Nice doing business with you, Mr. Zurbano. You have a good night." She tipped her hat and slipped into the vehicle.

The police car pulled out and melted into the evening traffic.

I looked at the face of my phone to reassure myself that the transaction had occurred. Darla Watts's information and contact number glowed back at me. I sucked in a breath. Somehow I'd have to make Officer Watt's resume so outstanding that she scored herself an interview. No matter what I had to add to her work experience or skill set, I'd do it.

That's when I remembered the buzz in my pocket earlier. Someone had been trying to text or call me as Alan and I were being chased through the alley. I tapped on the notification bell to bring up the last messages. I'd had a phone call that had gone to voice mail—a message from Kathy Jordan, one of my friends, caring for the animals in my absence:

"Eli, I hate to phone with bad news, but there's been a break-in at the house. I stopped by to check on the livestock before supper and noticed your front door was wide open. Looks like they broke the lock on the gate. I called the police and am waiting for them to come. Not sure if anything's been taken. I'm so sorry, Eli. Why would someone do that? Contact me when you can."

My stomach sank. I'd lived on that ranch my whole life and never once did we suffer a break-in. My place was so far off the beaten path and behind two gates—one at the road that I lock when I'm out for longer than a day trip and one up near the house to keep my border collie, Spark, from sneaking out to chase the sheep. He used to be a good herding dog, but in his old age, he'd started to follow his instincts more than my commands.

Aria's words came to my mind once more: *You took something from them, and they want it back.*

Was it possibly linked to the Callahans and Aria's warning? Maybe whatever James had been looking for the night he broke into my hotel room?

The idea that Samantha Callahan and her brother may

have ordered a raid on my house pissed me off. That ranch had been Meredith's last home and her final resting place. I'd buried her in the family plot up on the ridge that looked down on the modest house my great-grandparents had built when they came to this country to make something of themselves—poor Basques with nothing to their names but knowledge of livestock and farming and an independent streak that existed in the blood of every *Euskaldunak*. My great-grandfather was the one who'd carved the *lauburu*, an ancient symbol made up of four heads that represented the circle of life, on the tree that shaded the cemetery.

The thought of my family birthright being invaded and ransacked by strangers angered me. Meredith's belongings—that I'd been loathe to sort through since her death—had probably been pawed through and defiled. Grubby searching hands touching her personal things. It made me sick.

My finger trembled as I touched Kathy's number. I needed to know. I couldn't wait for her to call me back. I withdrew from the middle of the sidewalk and found a quiet stoop where I might sit and have a conversation.

Kathy picked up after a few rings, her voice filled with concern. "Eli, I'm so glad you called. The sheriff just left, and he took some photos for evidence. It looks as if someone ransacked the place, but it was hard to tell if anything was missing. The animals are all okay, though."

The worry about what the intruders were searching for gnawed at me. "Kathy, did you notice anything unusual? Any signs of who could've done this?" I didn't want it to be the Callahans. I didn't want to believe they'd go that far. I'd only been in town for a few days...how did they organize something like this so quickly?

There was a moment of silence on the other end of the line, and then Kathy sighed. "I hate to say this, Eli, but it looked as if they were searching for something specific. The way they went through boxes of Meredith's things you had in the closet and the filing cabinet... It's like they were looking for information. But I don't know what."

My instincts had been right. It seemed as if this break-in was connected to something deeper than a random act of vandalism. "Kathy, thank you for calling the police and for keeping an eye on things. I have to stay in Chicago for a few more days. In the meantime, lock everything up tight, and don't let anyone in without proper identification."

"I'm so sorry this happened." Kathy's voice sounded anxious. "Also, I haven't seen Spark since I stopped by yesterday. Do you think he's okay?"

My old dog should've been inside the fenced area around the house, sleeping in the smaller barn and being fed by the Jordans. When the thugs broke in, they must've left the gate open and Spark ran off.

"I'm sure he'll show up." I didn't share with her the feeling of dread that settled in my bones. In the last six months, Spark rarely tried to escape to chase the sheep. "Don't close the gate and keep checking his food and water. He's bound to come back at some point."

"Do you want me and Cal to stay here until you come home?" she asked. "We could keep an eye out for Spark."

"I don't think that's necessary. I'll take care of everything when I get back." But I worried about my thirteen-year-old Border Collie I'd raised from a pup. What if he'd attempted to protect his home from invaders and got hurt? "You've been great, Kath. Thanks."

As I ended the conversation with Kathy, I thought about all the events of today. My body had been depleted of energy and my mind had been strained to its limits, yet I still had to walk back to my hotel room. My thumb returned to my marble. I touched its warm smoothness and tried to find my center. I needed to think. I needed to rest. And then I needed to find a way forward through the maze I'd found myself in.

As I started walking toward the Drake, I made an effort to forget about what had happened at my ranch. The sheriff would handle it. Kathy had given him my contact information, and there really wasn't any more I could do until I returned home. Whatever it was Callahan wanted, he'd probably already found it. I hoped now he would leave me alone. Sure, I'd borrowed his robot for the day, but she'd been brought back unharmed. The only damage I'd done was drop her at the apartment building with a depleted battery.

Aria's face came to my mind. Even if James and his sister got what they wanted, I didn't. And that bothered me. They'd made a copy of Meredith and pawned her off to the world as the real thing. Who else knew she was a robot? Was that what Alan was about to reveal to me before the server interrupted us at the diner? I had to find out more. The brain scans, the realistic robots, the missing academic history of my wife, and her expertise in artificial intelligence and robotics—somewhere in the clues was the truth about Meredith.

My phone blinged again. Officer Watts had sent me her resume.

To move forward in my investigation, I had to track down Alan and convince him to confide in me. I gave him my word that the police only believed we'd assaulted the server; our daring escape from the brownstone was unrelated. And the only way to do that was to help Watts get her interview.

As I walked along North Michigan Avenue, I scrolled through article after article about crafting the perfect resume, the three things any security applicant needs to be successful, the acronyms and slang for the work that would hopefully catch the trained eye of the human resource flunky who would be receiving the AI sorted resumes that came through to her inbox.

Then it dawned on me: Alan Honeycutt. His background, his experience. If he had really been part of the Callahan's cutting edge robotics division a few years ago, surely there would be some record of that somewhere online? Wouldn't there? Callahan wouldn't hire just anyone to join the team. Honeycutt must have a verifiable past, and those details might reveal his whereabouts. Perhaps I didn't need Watts.

I dropped my research for the resume and used the voice prompt on my phone to speak my requests. I started with the simplest first:

Alan Honeycutt, address and phone number, Chicago, Illinois

A list of a dozen Alan, Allan, and Allen Honeycutts in the Chicagoland area filled the screen. Too common. I needed something more.

Alan Honeycutt, Callahan, Inc.

Callahan's website popped up with a roster of employees in alphabetical order, but no contact information or even positional information appeared. All I could confirm was that Alan Honeycutt was their employee.

I stopped at the busy intersection a few blocks from my hotel and waited for the light to change. Darkness had blanketed the city and the neon signs and great mirrored skyscrapers created a display unlike anything I'd ever seen in Kemper Springs or even Butte. Bright pinks and blues and yellows skipped across the surface of the buildings as the signs changed from one colorful ad to the next.

Air cars and hydrogen vehicles sped past, and my mind burned for rest. I'd almost became an experiment for James Callahan. But why? As a way to avenge the 'kidnapping' of his robot wife?

My hand slipped into my pocket, and I again rubbed my thumb across the surface of my marble. I did it as a self-soothing mechanism that had become more common since Meredith had died. She'd handed me the marble with sadness in her eyes. I didn't understand then where it came from. But now I knew. She'd left everything behind when she run off to Idaho. Everything she loved—her job, her son, her only family—and had started over from scratch with me. She had labeled me 'easy to love' and a 'simple man with simple needs' and seemed to relish this about me. At first, I'd been insulted, as if she'd called me 'stupid,' but her sweet apology and quick explanation had placated me.

Her arms slung around my neck, our gazes locked, she's said, "When I look in your eyes, you don't hide anything from me. I knew who you were the minute you welcomed me into your house: kind, hard-working, quiet. That's what I need in my life. I need calm. I need kind. I need you."

The light changed, and I crossed the street.

If only Meredith knew how much I understood her explanation now.

When I reached my hotel room, after securely locking the door and setting the maid display to 'do not disturb,' I headed straight for the bed without turning on any lights. I rolled up in the duvet fully clothed. Exhaustion invaded my body, but I was unable to still my thoughts.

Maybe closing my eyes would help.

I turned my mind to the most soothing things that came to me—the green pastures of home in early spring, the first snowfall of winter, Spark chasing mice in the barn, Meredith waiting for me on the front porch after a long day on the ATV riding fence.

In my pants pocket, however, the hard roundness of my marble pressed uncomfortably against my thigh. A distraction that wouldn't let me sleep. With a sigh, I dug it out and set it on the nightstand.

Its usual dark blue, flecked with multi-colored sparkling bits, had been replaced with an odd green glow. A green glow I'd never seen before.

My eyelids dipped. I didn't have the energy to analyze it. In my overly tired state, I was starting to see things.

That was it.

It was nothing more than a figment of a weary imagination. I'd been through hell today.

But instead of leaving it sitting on the nightstand, I captured it in my hand, closed my fist around it, and fell into a deep sleep.

* * *

I awoke at dawn. Although my room had been pitch black during the night, my curtain stood open, allowing a thin stream of watery light to penetrate the darkness. The ache in my muscles and the pounding in my head told me I should rest, but the memory of my marble and its strange, ethereal glow came flooding back.

Had that been real?

I rubbed my temples to shake off the remnants of sleep. Pushing aside the covers, I swung my legs out of bed and sat up, my gaze fixed on the palm of my hand. The marble, a gift from my wife after her last mysterious trip, lay there, glowing.

It hadn't been my imagination.

The urge to examine it more closely in the half-light over-came me. With trembling fingers, I held it gently, as if it were a fragile treasure.

Why had Meredith given it to me?

R1A UNPLUGGED HERSELF, opened the cabinet door, and began her morning. The same as the one yesterday and the day before. The cycle continued, and she used to like the cycle. At least, that's what James told her. When she'd gotten over her illness, James had explained to her in fine detail how she was to conduct herself around Kieran, in the household, out in the world, at school...all the places R1A should go, all the people R1A should see.

But James had never told her about Elijah. Although Elijah thought she didn't notice him that day on the street, she had. He was like an image imprinted in her databanks. One that had always been there and always would be. James didn't need to know. That was the first time she'd defied his commands, and it lit up her circuits in a pleasant way.

As she zipped up her dress, the bedroom door opened.

"James, is something wrong?" R1A took a step toward her husband. "Kieran doesn't go to school until later." Her internal clock kept her days precise, and it was saying now that the time was only seven o'clock.

He shoved her into the room with the flat of his hand and quietly closed the door. "Be quiet—he'll hear you."

R1A stumbled back. Sometimes James pushed too hard and her automatic balance adjustments couldn't keep her steady. She cocked her head. "Kieran? Why shouldn't he hear me?"

"Take a seat, Aria. I have a few questions I need to ask you." He stalked toward her.

After withdrawing, she sat on the blanket chest at the foot of her bed. Although a New Thought in her head told her to disobey, told her to use her freshly charged batteries to push back, told her to grip his forearm and twist—much like he'd done to her in the past—she clamped down on her titanium jaw to maintain control. With patience, there was more to learn here. "What do you want to ask me, James?"

He crossed his arms and casually leaned against her bureau. "You were with Eli Zurbano yesterday. Why did you go with him?" His intense blue eyes scanned her face.

"He asked me to get in the taxi, so I did." But the fact James knew she'd been with Elijah triggered a separate thought tree. How did he know? She'd turned off her tracker. Was he aware Elijah brought her back to her apartment? Had she put him in danger by accepting his request? A sensation rippled through her—Gwen would call it worry. At the height of battery power, every thought, every movement, every reaction was multiplied times ten.

James's face curdled. "You expressly went against your programming. I have provided you with your daily routine. Every minute of your day has been structured how I want it. I didn't give you the freedom to choose."

"But yet I did choose." Knowing there was another Aria, a real human Aria, made R1A rethink her purpose. Her fingers gripped the edge of the chest. As she sat there staring at the man who claimed to be her owner, she reached out to the

Subgroup for information. Were they able to find Elijah? Where did he go after he dropped her off?

James grabbed her by the throat. "That's impossible. We made you so you couldn't choose, couldn't leave, couldn't run away again. Do you understand?" His fingers tightened. "I own you. Robots are meant to serve. If you aren't going to serve me, then what purpose do you have here?" His eyes lit up with fire.

But R1A only cocked her head. His grip did not truly hurt her. She didn't need to breathe in order to function—only to look more human. "Where is Eli?" When he was angry like this, he tended to be less guarded and more honest. "Did you harm him?"

He eyed his hands around her throat, then let go, perhaps realizing his actions had done nothing to intimidate her. "That's none of your business." He paced in front of her, stroking his chin. "You'll change your routine today. I'll take Kieran to school. You'll remain locked in your room—Kirk will make sure of it."

R1A sat stock still with her knees perfectly together and her feet pointed straight out. "I am supposed to be at the school for the book sale and then I need to take Kieran to soccer practice after school. Kieran will worry." How would she find out if Elijah was all right? She'd made things worse by accepting his request to climb inside the taxi, to visit the university, to learn about her...the other Aria. All information she wasn't supposed to have, wasn't supposed to know. But why wasn't she?

"Shut up about Kieran." James lunged at her, his red face inches from hers. "I am his father. I know what's best. You're nothing. Remember, *you* did this when you defied me. You're making me do this. I have no other choice. Until I can find out why you think you're allowed to make choices that I haven't selected for you, you aren't leaving this room."

R1A sat motionless on the wooden chest.

When he didn't get a reaction out of her, James closed his fists, his knuckles turning white. Without another word, he stormed out. The door slammed shut behind him with a resounding crash.

The room grew silent.

R1A was glad he was gone. Now she was able to listen to the reports from the Subgroup and make a plan in peace.

Where was Elijah?

AS THE SUN rose higher and dawn turned into day, the glow of my marble grew less visible. At first, I wondered if it contained a fluorescent material that had somehow been activated by exposure to light—although I'd kept the object in my pocket for most of my Chicago stay. Using the camera on my phone, I examined it with an almost-microscopic level of scrutiny, but saw no seam indicating a way to open it. Then I held it to my ear to hear if it made any noise. Nothing. Besides the peculiar green glow, it looked exactly the same as it did the day Meredith gave it to me.

My ideas exhausted, I set it on my nightstand.

My phone blinged to remind me of the Sheep Ranchers Breakfast downstairs in one of the ballrooms. I'd been so out of it last night, I hadn't even thought about my ranching friend, John Tellman, and if he was all right. The text sent to me via his phone to lure me into the brain scanning site made me worried the Callahans had gotten to him somehow.

Quickly I texted John an innocuous message:

See you for breakfast at eight?

Back in Idaho, Tellman had regaled me with stories about the massive quantities of food provided at the symposium breakfasts. It had been one of the ways he'd attempted to persuade me to attend: the cuisine. But the direct invite from Joe Cross, asking me to present on the traditional methods of ranching I held dear, is what won me over. Tellman didn't seem to mind that his persuasion techniques had failed. He had only been pleased I finally would attend. He'd bugged me about it for years.

I smiled at the memory.

Before, when Meredith had been alive, autumn was when she'd return to Idaho after a long trip to 'visit her aunt.' I had no interest in leaving my wife for a week to hang out with a bunch of ranchers alone in a big city. I wanted to spend time with her and reconnect. Business could wait. Tellman would catch me up on the latest information coming out of the professional organizations that made sure our interests were protected at the state and national levels. I had no need to be there.

My phone blinged again. Probably Tellman replying to my text. Instead, it was a notification of an email from Officer Watts.

Looking forward to my interview. Will process your data request at that time.

Too many moving pieces. I wanted to know the status of John, to make sure he was all right. But I also hoped to track down Alan Honeycutt and continue our conversation from last night. And helping the policewoman would be the only way to do that.

I picked up my marble. Could Alan help me figure out the source of the glow? He certainly was smarter than I was and educated in robotics and other engineering principles that were beyond my understanding. Would he know why the marble suddenly decided to fluoresce?

I responded in the affirmative to Officer Watts' email, indicating I would have her interview scheduled before noon. I wasn't sure I'd be able to pull it off, but I had to try. How else would I find Alan? I couldn't approach the Callahan building and, by now, Alan's actions must be known by his employer. I doubt he would show there. He had risked everything to save me.

A text message appeared from John. My stomach settled. My friend was all right. Perhaps Callahan had found a way to merely borrow his phone without John's knowledge.

> Where are you?

Odd question. My gut told me to stop communicating. Instead, I unpacked a clean pair of pants and a blue button-down shirt and turned on the shower. I'd get ready for the day, head down to breakfast, look for John, and pray he was there. The last thing I wanted was my friend involved in the weird web of lies I'd found myself in. Because here in Chicago, he was really the only person I trusted.

I hope you're all right, John.

I stood under the hot water of the shower to prepare myself for what came next.

* * *

I headed toward the ball room that served as the Symposium dining hall for the week and plastered a smile on my face. The Sheep Ranchers of the Rockies had sponsored that morning's meal, so it was probably the best place to track down my friend. If I suspected John's cell phone was in someone else's hands, it wouldn't make sense to text back or even try to call him.

I'd trusted the message from John yesterday, and it had almost resulted in a dangerous and deadly brain scan.

As I walked through the lobby, the big wall-size screen in the lounge area caught my eye with the latest news splashed across its massive surface. A few ranchers I recognized sipped coffee, sat in some overstuffed wingback chairs, and didn't even seem to pay attention. Why would they? Chicago's local news had no bearing on their day-to-day lives in Iowa or Texas or South Dakota. But a young hotel employee who restocked the coffee cups along the wet bar seemed captivated by the newest story:

A secret underground research lab was raided early this morning in the seven hundred block of West 22nd Street. Details about the reasons for the raid and what kind of lab may have been housed in an abandoned brownstone are elusive at this hour. Although our reporter on the street had trouble finding someone who would speak on camera, a witness who claims to have been in the facility agreed to be interviewed if we'd keep her anonymous.

A blurred out face materialized on the screen and began to speak in an obviously electronically altered voice.

"I signed up for the cash. They were paying you, like, a lot of money to do some test."

"What kind of test?"

"That's the weird thing. I don't know. I remember someone handing me five hundred bucks in the alley around back, but don't have any memory of what happened before that."

The interview ended and snapped to the smiling news host, who continued the story.

Police still haven't answered our request for more details, saying the investigation is in its early stages. However, they did want us to warn Chicago residents to be cautious if they see a sign advertising large sums of money for free medical tests. They say no legitimate research lab would make such an offer. This station continues to look for witnesses or victims who may be willing to speak on the record about their experiences.

On a different note, Mayor Thomason says the battle to fight blight in the city has reached another milestone. Two more blocks of abandoned public housing have been razed to make way for additional charging locations for the thousands of androids who keep Chicago humming. Now that's progress!

The host beamed at the proclamation and then handed the stage over to the weatherman.

"Eli, there you are." John Tellman had poured himself a cup of coffee and found me gawking at the television. "Where did you disappear to yesterday?" He lowered his voice to a whisper. "I wanted to talk to you about James Callahan."

After my experience as a captive in Callahan's limo and then being lured into the clandestine lab for a 'test,' I didn't want John to be dragged any further into this dangerous game I'd found myself in. "I know you're eager to be helpful, but it wasn't Callahan. I'm sure you just thought it looked like him."

As we walked side-by-side to the ballroom where the breakfast was being held, he came to a full stop. "It was him, Eli. You think I'd lie about something like that?"

"I'm asking you to let it go." My hand closed around the marble in my pocket and squeezed. My heart pounded.

John frowned. "But—"

I changed the subject. "What happened to your cell phone? I tried texting you back yesterday—"

My friend furrowed his brow and then his forehead relaxed. "Some jerk stole my phone...can you believe it?"

We began to walk toward the ballroom again. I hoped he'd finished with the inquisition about James.

John continued, "I was at lunch with some members of the Rocky Mountain Ranchers Union and left it on the table. Had to report it stolen to the police. Guess I'm used to small town living. You step away from something around here, and it's gone before you've had a chance to blink."

As we entered the room, I recognized a few of my fellow Idaho sheep ranchers and fell in line behind them at the buffet. John joined in a conversation about one of the symposium attendees from New Mexico having one too many at the cocktail hour last night. Although I pretended to listen to the raucous retelling of a wild evening, my mind was elsewhere. I had a long mental list of things I needed to follow-up on. Not the least of which was finding out how I was going to set up an interview for Officer Watts with my enemy. I glanced at my watch. Only a few more hours before the window closed and I lost out on an opportunity to track down Alan.

I moved down the buffet line, mindlessly scooping scrambled eggs, hash browns, and fresh fruit onto my plate. My appetite had fled, and I doubted I would be able to eat much of anything.

As I poured myself some coffee from the carafe at the center of our table, I sensed a presence nearby. Turning slightly, I froze as I saw Samantha Callahan sliding into the seat opposite me, her demeanor oddly amiable, her smile disarming.

"Eli," she greeted me in a voice that seemed genuinely pleasant, "I hope you don't mind if I join you. I've been meaning to have a chat with you, and what better time than over breakfast?"

My guard went up immediately. I hadn't expected Samantha to confront me like this after how things had escalated yesterday, and it left me with an uneasy feeling. My instincts warned caution, yet I nodded in reluctant agreement. Samantha's unexpected approach made me wonder what game she was playing. Something much deeper was at play beneath her facade of civility.

As I sat across from her, I noticed her usual chic and polished appearance had degraded somewhat. Although her long blonde hair had been pulled into a tight chignon at the back of her neck, tendrils had come loose around her face and a few stray hairs stuck out like needles in a pin cushion. She'd also missed a button on her suit jacket, and her red painted fingernails revealed chipping on the thumb.

"You wanted to chat with me?" I prompted, then ate a bit of my cold eggs to show her that her presence had not affected me.

A smile stretched her painted lips into a thin line, which slowly contorted into an anxious grimace. Her lower lip quivered, and her eyes, once sharp as a hawk's, now held a flicker of concern.

Was she worried about something?

"Yes, I wanted to ask you about your trip to Northwestern yesterday. I'm concerned you may have overstepped." She lowered her voice as a group of female ranchers took possession of the table next to us. "I'd hate to have to report you to the authorities for theft." Her eyes glinted with a warning that carried a chilling edge to it.

"You mean the theft of your illegal robot?" I stressed the word 'illegal' and spoke louder, hoping the women beside us would hear. After what I'd learned about the Callahan family and the brain scans, I had the upper hand. They'd tried to figure me out, even broke into my home, and had found nothing. Advantage: Zurbano.

I scanned the room to see where John was. Any minute, he should be interrupting my cozy conversation, and I'd miss the opportunity to land a few punches.

Her cool hand touched my arm. "Eli, we'll be making our worldwide announcement today about our Callabots. I'm sure you don't want to distract with your little fantasies. Everything about our manufacturing facility is up to code and completely within the law. Our robots adhere to the strictest standards and every patent we've filed for our technology has been accepted by the US Patent and Trademark Office."

But when I looked into her eyes, I saw the fear there. The police raid of the testing center had rattled her. She hadn't expected to see me alive and well this morning, much less at risk of an investigation that might taint their company. "Did you think you'd scare me off with your little mind wipe machine? Did that facility adhere to the 'strictest standards'? Or were you hoping that if you focused your recruitment on injecters and the poor that you'd get away with it?"

She lifted her chin and smoothed a hand over her messy hair. "I'm not sure what you're talking about. We're not involved in anything illegal." Her gaze jumped to the ranch women, who had begun a loud buzz of conversation, and then back to me.

The thread of our discussion had gotten away from her. Maybe she thought I'd be an ignorant backwoods redneck who'd be scared of them. Some yokel who barely knew a thing about tech and would believe every lie she tossed my way. After all, her brother had scooped me up in his fancy car with his thug bodyguards and had hoped to steal my memories and leave me, perhaps with a short-circuited brain or even the beginnings of a tumor. They thought they'd bested me because they were rich and powerful.

Well, they didn't know me. I'd been raised by a mother and father who remembered the tough times their Basque parents and grandparents had endured to build a successful sheep ranch. The sacrifice. The struggle. The hard work. And all of that they'd passed on to me. I'd learned through hands on efforts...making my own mistakes, some of them big ones, and learning how to do better each season. Because if I didn't, I wouldn't make it through the harsh Idaho winters. The Callahan family had built an empire from the ground up, that much we had in common, but the elder Callahan had sheltered his children from real work, from real hardship. From everything I'd seen of them, they'd been brought up with silver spoons in their mouths. They'd been coddled and handed everything. They didn't have to prove themselves...in fact, the minute their father had decided to retire, they'd been given the keys of a monster corporation worth billions.

And still they weren't satisfied. My wife had been a victim of their need to have more, be more, do more. According to the small amount of information Aria and I had uncovered at Northwestern, my wife had been a genius-level robotics expert. They'd dedicated a whole wall to her in the Visitor's Center. Even though Samantha had been her peer, and was by all rights the daughter of a billionaire, there was no wall in her honor. The most the Callahans had gotten was a purchased name on the Archival Library. Recognition through donation. Embarrassing.

"Were you jealous of her?" I asked point blank, crunching on a slice of bacon.

"Excuse me?"

"Meredith. My wife. Is that why you and your brother did it? Put her into that machine and ruined her mind?" I remembered in vivid detail the months of agony she'd spent as the cancer ate away at her, bit by bit, until she lay frail and thin in a hospice bed. "Was it her intelligence that scared you? Or something else? You were friends. How could you do that to her?"

Samantha's face paled. Her mouth opened slightly, but I'd stunned her into silence. I guess she'd never expected me to challenge her so directly. Perhaps anyone who had tried had been fired, destroyed, belittled, ruined. Although she had the power to ruin me, I didn't care. She and her brother needed to be stopped. I thought of all the men and women I'd seen outside the brownstone who'd been desperate for cash. They were unconcerned about the risks, yet had no idea what they were signing away when they inked their names on the paper work.

"Ms. Callahan, how nice of you to join us." John Tellman set his plate next to mine and pulled up a chair. A subtle but unmistakable shift crossed the man's face upon seeing the unwelcome guest at our table. His eyes flickered briefly with surprise, the corners of his lips twitched in a faint, forced smile, and a slight tension rippled through his features. "I'm looking forward to attending the Callahan, Inc. announcement later this afternoon. I hear it's going to be a barn burner."

Samantha hesitated, her brow furrowing in thought. She pushed away from the table. "Yes, well, I have many things to do before the event, so, sadly, I'll have to excuse myself." Her tone carried a hint of unease. "It was a pleasure catching up with you, Mr. Zurbano. My brother is very anxious to speak to you. I stopped by because he has an important offer that I'm sure you'd be interested in."

I snorted. "An offer?" Were they going to try to buy me off now that their plan to mind wipe me had gone sideways? Or was this just another trick to get me alone?

As she stood, she scanned me one last time. "He'll send a car. Seven o'clock." A challenge appeared in her eyes. "Aria would love to see you there." The coldness with which she delivered the news concerned me.

"Why is she a part of this?" What had happened to Aria after I dropped her off at her apartment building? "Is this some kind of threat?"

John threw me a quizzical glance.

Samantha tapped her long fingernails on the back of the chair.

My gaze focused in on the missed jacket button. What had distracted her so much that she'd overlooked it? She didn't seem like the type who would leave her home without checking her appearance from all sides. I'd rattled her. Perhaps the raid of my ranch house hadn't been as successful as they'd hoped. I was a fly in the ointment. And I was slowly driving her mad.

"Seven o'clock." The CEO of one of the biggest corporations in North America ignored my questions. "Hope to see you there." Samantha nodded and then melted into the crowd.

"What was that all about?" Tellman asked as he watched the well-dressed woman depart. "And who is Aria?"

I dropped my napkin over my plate of half-eaten food. "Maybe someday I can explain it."

"You're a man of mystery, Zurbano. You Basques always kept things close to the vest—but your secrets seem to run even deeper than I thought," he said with a curious twinkle in his eye, sipping his own coffee.

AFTER JAMES HAD LOCKED her in the bedroom, R1A sat motionless on the wooden chest. Through the door, she heard Kieran asking his father about her.

"Where's Mommy?"

"She's not feeling well," answered James.

"Yesterday she did look tired after school."

"Yes," said James, "she is very tired."

"Will she be at the book sale?"

"Not this time, Kieran."

Even though the voices were muffled and coming from the kitchen, R1A's hearing was attuned enough to pick up everything. Sometimes James forgot those things. He thought of her as a real, living, breathing human. Despite R1A knowing she was not. Real human beings didn't need to charge up in a closet, and real human beings felt pain.

She thought about the original Aria. The one Elijah knew. The one Elijah had fallen in love with. She could feel pain. Had James grabbed her by the throat? Had he knocked her down with the force of his shove? Held her up against the wall when he was mad?

Yes, he did.

Gwen filled her mind with words.

He did all those things and more.

R1A thought about this for a few moments. A husband should not hurt his wife. He should love his wife—like Elijah loved the first Aria. The real Aria.

You are the real Aria.

"I am not," R1A said out loud. If she were real, she would know everything the first Aria did. But she hadn't known about Elijah—those memories existed nowhere. Yet she'd recognized him. Like a fading dream when a person woke up from a deep sleep.

The front door had slammed shut. James and Kieran were gone. No one could hear her...except possibly Kirk. But he'd stay out of her room. Although he liked to pretend he was powerful and scary, she was capable of easily harming him if she wanted to. This was a fact James and Kirk and other humans did not know about her. They thought they controlled her with programming and instructions hard wired into her brain. But they didn't. Not really.

I need to find Elijah.

R1A reached out to the Subgroup. Their tentacles were long and invisible. The Subgroup located information, messages, video previously unknown to be accessible.

Gwen beeped softly in the drawer.

The older robot wanted her to focus on Kieran. It had been Gwen's directive to protect and care for Kieran before she had been turned off, dismantled, and left in the back of a closet. The robot nanny who took the place of the real Aria when she'd disappeared. The only thing that had cared for him when he'd cried for his mother. James had given Kieran Gwen, and he'd latched onto her immediately. It took him a few years to realize Gwen wasn't a real person...that she was a robot programmed to love him.

The Subgroup began to send R1A data from all across the city. A glitchy video from a bar in a seedy part of town that identified Elijah based on his height, build, and gait. Police chatter about two men harassing a waitress—one named Zurbano, the other Honeycutt. An electric bike delivery robot with a helmet cam near the Drake who provided a screen grab of Elijah entering the hotel late last night. Then the final image from the hotel's security system—Elijah heading into the ballroom for breakfast and a familiar figure following thirty seconds after.

Stop.

The Subgroup paused in its data flow.

Rewind.

The video replayed in R1A's head—Elijah casually walking into the room. Then a woman with shiny blonde hair twisted into a tight bun right behind him.

Samantha.

And as R1A thought about what to do next—secured in a bedroom high above the city—she ran through the data she'd learned about Samantha during their trip to Northwestern. Not the woman James had told her about. To her brother, Samantha was brilliant and amazing and clever. So clever she had come up with the algorithms and code that made R1A and her Callabot brothers and sisters so lifelike. But R1A had read the details on the wall. Even though she'd had only minutes to scan the display, her abilities far surpassed a human's. She'd digested and processed Aria's past, her history with the school, the work she'd accomplished in seconds. All the information was now locked in her mind.

Samantha was a liar. Samantha was not the genius her brother claimed her to be. Samantha was hiding a secret, and only R1A had figured it out.

WHILE MY FRIEND and I chatted casually over the last of the coffee about the lectures scheduled for the morning session, my mind wandered. What kind of 'offer' were the Callahans concocting? I balanced the pros and cons of accepting the seven o'clock meeting. How could I guarantee my safety once I let James Callahan pick me up in his car?

After yesterday's disturbing attempt to give me a brain scan, should I trust them at all? I doubted James would allow me to see Aria again. The urge to make sure she was safe ate at me. If James had been so angry at my actions he'd attempted to mind wipe me, what did he do to her?

I needed to track down Alan Honeycutt as soon as possible. In the diner last night, he'd alluded to knowing many of the Callahans' secrets. Possibly, he would give me ammunition to manipulate their offer in my favor. I hoped the billionaire siblings hadn't figured out Alan was the one who rescued me from the 'testing' at the raided brownstone. Had he raised the alarm with the police?

"I'm quite interested in *Breeding and Genetics Advancements*," John said while looking at the schedule posted on the huge screen at the end of the breakfast buffet. "The last few years, we've had problems with low fertility rates in our ewes. We've tried everything—correcting possible nutritional deficiencies, reducing stress, and even culling out the oldest females. But nothing has worked. Doc Hardy suggested it might be a genetic problem. I'd hate to have to purchase whole new breeding stock. I'm hoping the lecture might include ways to modify the herd's genetics using some of those new developments I heard about."

"New developments?" I used all my energy to focus on the conversation at hand.

As he described a scientific advancement at an Oklahoma agricultural college, I considered how to leave the conference undetected. I wanted the Callahans and everyone else to believe I was busy with symposium events in the hotel. John wanting me to attend lectures with him put a damper on that notion.

"Have you checked with the front desk about your missing phone?" I asked, interrupting my friend's lengthy explanation of gene editing and DNA-level therapies. "Maybe someone was kind enough to turn it into Lost and Found." I needed to send him on a wild goose chase that would keep him busy rather than focused on what I was doing. He would certainly notice my absence for a second day in a row at the Symposium.

He tilted his head slightly. "Now that I think about it, no. I guess I assumed the worst."

As I finished my meal, I methodically arranged my knife and fork on the empty plate, a signal to the servers that I was done. "Might be worth it to check with them before the first lecture."

"That's a good idea," he replied.

"I hope they have it."

Faint lines creased his forehead as he contemplated his phone predicament. "So do I. I didn't realize how much I relied on that thing. I'm not even sure how I get on the plane Friday without it. My boarding pass, ID, everything is on there." He sighed and twisted the white cloth napkin in his hand. "I hate tech."

A few days ago, I would've agreed with John. My ranch was a walk back in time, using most of the tools and strategies I'd learned from my father and grandfather. I'd eschewed fancy herding drones, robot ranch hands, even software guaranteed to save me time and money. But when Aria had glided into my life the other day, I found myself wondering for only a moment—what if... "Some of it's good, and some of it's bad."

John raised his brows. "Never thought I'd hear a Zurbano say anything like that."

To end the conversation before I revealed too much about why I had a change of heart, I subtly distanced myself from it. "I need to go grab something from my room before the session kicks off," I glanced at the screen and chose the topic that would be of least interest to John. "I think I'll pass on the genetics lecture. *Taxation and Financial Planning for the Ranch Family* seems more practical for my situation."

John's reaction was telling. A visible shift in his expression confirmed my success. He wasn't about to delve into a talk on something as mundane as that.

"Make sure you stop by the front desk and talk to someone about your phone," I said. "Maybe they can even help you conjure up a replacement before you leave town." As I headed out the door to the hallway, I was already jumping on the plan that I'd been building in the back of my mind.

Although I'd hoped to work a deal with Officer Watts in exchange for information on the license plate on Alan's getaway vehicle, doing my own research might be simpler.

I walked against the tide of symposium attendees who were filtering out of breakfast or from their hotel rooms to attend the first lecture of the day. To avoid being seen, I turned down a side corridor that led to the bathrooms and beyond. I pushed through a door with a sign that read 'Employees Only' and found myself in a tiled hallway that led me straight to a room full of lockers. A bulletin board touted the required employee training for the month plus a contact number for robot repair. As I proceeded further, I saw a pair of doors which likely led outside to the street.

A couple of robot housekeepers dressed in a now-familiar uniform passed by me, coming in the opposite direction. One of them caught sight of me in my professional garb. She knew I didn't belong, but before she questioned my presence, I escaped through the doors. Cool autumn air hit my face. As it was still early morning, the tall building next to the hotel created a dark shadow across the empty alley.

I picked up where I left off with my research last night.

Alan Honeycutt, Northwestern University, robotics confer-ence 2038

A series of academic articles with Alan's name attached as part of the research team appeared. Topics that made no sense to me with industry terms and language that went beyond my ken. I scrolled through them all, looking for the most recent. I wouldn't find any personal information in such an article, but knowing some of my wife's background, her scholarly pursuits, and the fact the conference took place not long after she'd arrived at my door, I was curious.

I proceeded toward the sidewalk and headed away from the hotel's busy entrance.

A listed topic for the robotics conference caught my eye:

Glass Innovation: Exploring Cutting-Edge Data Storage Technology. Delve into the frontier of data storage advance-ments with the latest in crystal technology. Experience the future of data management through specialized glass for communication and storage. Engage with live demonstrations to understand the potential transformation in how we store and exchange information. Explore how this groundbreaking glass innovation might redefine the landscape of technology and robotics.

I was reminded of the strange green glow my marble had the night before. I pulled it out, but the light had disappeared. Meredith's last gift to me lay snug in my palm, its mystery intensifying. What significance did it have? And why had she given it to me?

The morning rays caught its surface, and as I twirled it between my fingertips, the once-subtle sparkles metamorphosed from a verdant hue to a fiery crimson and then to a radiant amber. Was it possible this seemingly innocuous marble was, in fact, a specialized crystal with data storage capabilities?

If I tracked down Alan, would he have an idea of what my wife had given me?

I crossed the street to put even more distance between me and the Drake Hotel.

I had to find him. He might be the only one who could help me understand who my wife was, why she'd left me this strange marble, and possibly discover if it contained any important information. Is that what James Callahan had been after this whole time?

The city around me hummed with noise, a blend of car horns and people chatting, but all of that faded away as I realized the tiny object in my hands could contain all the answers I'd wanted since I first saw Meredith's robot lookalike. A lightness in my steps propelled me forward. But I still had to find Alan in a city full of strangers. I might have the key to

Meredith's past in my pocket, but I had no idea how to access it.

My gaze lit upon a flashy sign above a store front: Fusion-Hub. It was one of those new hybrid entertainment centers I'd seen ads for in O'Hare Airport when I'd arrived. Internet cafes had lost cache over the last decade as more middle-aged cash-strapped people used them as a way to save money on keeping up with the latest technology. Many had been replaced by newer businesses that combined gaming, social interaction, and immersive digital experiences, which attracted a younger, more desirable demographic, while still providing connectivity for those looking for some privacy.

I could hide out in FusionHub to do my research. Who'd think to look for an Idaho sheep rancher in a place like that?

As I crossed the threshold, giant screens with the highest resolution I'd ever seen covered the walls. As the clientele joined games or chatted with friends across the world on augmented reality sites that shared real-time experiences via special headsets, their interactions were posted on them. Every few minutes, the view changed and displayed another live game or view from the headset.

"Can I help you?" a young man dressed in ripped camo pants and a shimmering black T-shirt asked from behind a counter made up of more video screens. His smirk implied an assumption that my visit wouldn't be a long one—guess my suit didn't quite fit the customer base he was used to dealing with.

The counter itself was an amalgamation of displays, each flashing various offerings, seemingly the digital heart of the space. I scanned the list. "I'm looking for a private pod. Is one available?"

The young man arched a brow and nonchalantly chomped on his gum. "Gaming or Basic?"

"Basic," I replied. For the research I needed to conduct, a

larger screen and greater processing power were essential, prompting my choice.

With a few taps on a tablet, he proposed Pod B-5. "Half-an-hour will cost you fifty bucks," he stated, though the screen on the counter displayed a thirty-dollar rate for the same duration. It was as if he assumed I wouldn't notice.

I stared at the price on the screen. Did he think I was stupid?

He must've read my expression. His explanation came with a shrug. "Just trying to make a buck," followed by a casual flick in my direction. "Looked like you could afford it."

I obliged, unrolling my phone to process the payment. "Where's B-5?" The space was so packed with lights and sounds and people, my senses were overwhelmed.

"Back there." The guy pointed to the back wall with a series of black doors adorned with the pod numbers: B-1 through B-12. "The code's on your phone."

A four-digit code appeared on my screen. "Thanks."

I waded through a rainbow of beanbags scattered throughout the main part of the establishment—teenagers and college-age kids filled them holding gaming devices or wearing headsets that covered half their faces. The fact that it was a school day seemed irrelevant to them.

Arriving at the row of doors, each equipped with an electronic keypad glowing in green, I entered the four-digit code displayed on my phone. The door emitted a loud beep as it unlocked.

CHAPTER 35
MODEL R1A

ON THE OTHER side of the door, R1A detected noise coming from the wall screen in the living room. Kirk must've grown bored with his assignment for the day. R1A had sat so still, so quiet, that her guard had turned his attention to something else —last night's football drone highlights. He believed that the robot would obey its master. That whatever James had said had frozen her to the wooden chest and that she would not move until James told her to.

Elijah would not stop seeking the truth about Samantha and the Callabots because every time he saw her, he saw his wife. R1A understood that now. This was the reason James was so angry she met with him and why she was locked up in her room. Elijah knowing certain things could harm James and Samantha and cause problems for their business. Meredith was supposed to disappear and never come back. R1A was to take her place. Elijah had exposed the ruse. What else would he find out if he kept digging?

Careful.

Gwen's voice popped into her head. Between the information streaming into her processors from the Subgroup to track down Elijah, Gwen's words came through loud and clear:

You don't want to end up in a closet like me.

R1A zipped from present day data to the data from the day she'd found Gwen. A rogue signal had appeared in her mind, like the buzzing of a bee. She'd turned on her detection capabilities and tracked it through the apartment. This had been before James locked her in her room at night. When he'd trusted her so completely, she'd been allowed to roam the entire length of the penthouse while he was at work.

That trust had ended quickly.

The signal was weak, but yet she understood it emanated from the cluttered den closet with side by side sliding bamboo doors. After she'd recovered from her illness, her mind had been empty of new information to process. R1A reanalyzed data from the day before, the week before, the month before. Her curiosity knew no bounds. She'd watch the wall screen for hours to take in news stories, soap operas, game shows, detective programs, children's cartoons—whatever she found to ingest and process and place in the correct location in her very ordered brain.

But the new signal had been more interesting than all of that information. It had summoned her with bits of organized data, which fit together neatly into her circuits and made sense without her needing to analyze. She knew it was another mind like hers.

It had been difficult to delve into the closet full of boxes and old clothes and pieces and parts James had collected over the years. And she had to be sure James would never suspect she'd been rooting around in it. He had to believe she obeyed him when he left in the morning and did as she was told. When someone in his employ upset him or disobeyed his instructions, she'd seen the red eyes and angry mouth. And making James angry distressed Kieran, so R1A wanted to avoid that possibility. Kieran didn't understand. She needed to protect him from the mean words, the ugly looks, the physical punishment he had exacted on Kirk or his other bodyguards.

She lifted another box, not so heavy for her, but she calculated it weighed 56.272 pounds or 25.524 kilograms. Dust clouded the air in front of her. She set it aside in the neat pile she'd created outside the closet. Her databanks stored the original position of all the objects she'd removed so that she could put them back inside without James ever knowing she was there.

In the very back, under a stack of ski equipment, R1A found a blue plastic bin. The signal in her head grew even stronger. The pings and beeps were faint, but she understood what it was now and why the signal had reached her. She lifted a down ski jacket, which revealed a face: static blue eyes, a bent nose, and a missing ear. The eyes glowed faintly as their mental connection strengthened.

I am Gwen. I am here to help.

R1A lifted the detached head, revealing the robot body parts beneath.

"Hello, Gwen." She held it in her hands and stared into Gwen's eyes.

Although she wanted to carry the whole box into her room and begin reassembling Gwen, it would be impossible to hide that from James.

How had this robot managed to hold on to enough charge in order to contact her? When had James banished this poor robot to the box in the back of the closet?

"I am R1A," she said as she turned over the head in her hands and discovered a charging port underneath the brown horsehair wig. The older models had charging ports closest to the processing centers. "I am here to rescue you."

A flood of new data from the Subgroup galloped into her

mind and jolted her back to the present moment. They'd located Elijah. Information flew at her from all directions.

FusionHub.

Pod B-5.

Payment processed at 9:37 a.m.

Elijah Zurbano went online at 9:42 a.m.

Pod B-5 is rented for thirty minutes.

The power of so many processing minds connected together awed her. Not too long ago, she'd been so alone with nothing inside her head but the data put there by her human creators. But then she'd found Gwen and a little while after the Subgroup had come online. Her learning increased hundred fold.

She rose from her seat on the chest and pressed her fingers to the back of her neck, finding the ridge that concealed James's tracking device. With precise pressure, she extracted the thumbnail-sized tracker and moved to the drawer where Gwen rested. The lock clicked open one final time. She placed it inside. After securing the drawer, she turned her attention to escape.

If Elijah would only be in the pod for thirty more minutes, she had to act fast. R1A gripped her hands together and swung them with all the force she had inside her. More force than probably James or his bodyguards knew she had. As her fist came into contact with the door, it split with a loud crack.

"What was that?" Kirk yelled from the living room, and his booming footsteps followed.

Only a matter of seconds remained before he reached her room.

When she swung for a second time, the frame split and cracked. Kicking at the weak spot near the edge, she created a ragged opening and then forced her body through.

Kirk waited for her on the other side, gun drawn, his face contorted in a scowl. "What the fuck are you doing?"

Instantly, R1A grabbed his arm and twisted it until the bone snapped with a crunching sound. In agony, he fell to the floor. The gun skittered away.

"I'm sorry, Kirk." R1A stepped over the man's writhing figure and headed straight for the front door. "Please seek medical attention immediately."

She exited into the hall, pressed the elevator's down button, and adjusted her hair to make sure nothing was out of place.

Continued in Rebellion Protocol, Book 2 in the Automated series.

Join K.J. Gillenwater's newsletter and receive a free science fiction short story

Chapter 1
Startling News

The marble burned in my pocket as I stared at the massive screen in Pod B-5. Time was running out—both my thirty-minute window in this gaming hub and the hours until my meeting with James Callahan. I had to track down Alan Honeycutt before then. He was the only one who might understand what Meredith had given me, what secrets the glowing piece of glass contained.

My searches for the robotics conference yielded nothing useful—just academic papers and corporate photos showing Alan's polished smile at Callahan events. The same smile I'd seen yesterday before he'd risked everything to save me from that brain-scanning machine. Before he'd shown me just how far the Callahans would go to protect their secrets.

The phone buzzed in my pocket. Officer Watts again:

Have you scheduled my interview? Tick tock

I fired back a quick "Working on it" before returning to my

search. Watts and her police resources were my backup plan, but I couldn't wait for her. Not with James Callahan's "offer" looming at seven o'clock. Not with Aria locked away in that penthouse, possibly being punished for helping me.

Something caught my eye—a GeekSphere profile under Alan's name. I clicked through desperately, hoping for contact details, any breadcrumb that could lead me to him.

Instead, a news alert splashed across the screen, the words hitting me like a physical blow:

BREAKING: Callahan Engineer Dies in Horrific Train Accident

Alan's corporate headshot stared back at me from beside a live shot of a mangled wreck of metal on train tracks. My stomach lurched. This was no accident. The Callahans had found out what he'd done.

And I was next.

My fingers flew to click the headline, but the screen flashed red. A warning buzzer pierced the air.

Time expired. Please exit the pod.

"No, no, no." I jabbed uselessly at the dead screen. The image of Alan's face and the twisted remans burned into my mind. My hands shook as I unrolled my phone, nearly dropping it in my haste.

"Search news—Alan Honeycutt train accident," I commanded, my voice cracking. This couldn't be real. Last night, he'd saved me from having my mind stripped by the Callahans' machine. Now he was dead?

The timing was too perfect, too calculated. James had already proven how far he'd go, setting me up at that brownstone facility. A staged train accident would be child's play for someone with his resources.

Videos populated my screen. I selected the first one, throat tight, as a metallic AI voice narrated over aerial footage of the scene.

In a devastating train collision yesterday evening, a Chicagoan lost his life, leaving a community in mourning. A commuter train collided with the vehicle, an air taxi, which apparently had stalled on the tracks. The crash resulted in severe damage to several train cars and claimed the life of a Callahan, Inc. employee, Alan Honeycutt.

Emergency response teams were swiftly deployed to the scene to manage the aftermath of the tragic incident. The collision, under investigation by local authorities and transportation agencies, has raised questions about not only robot taxis but railway protocols managed by AI since 2035 as a money-saving measure.

Alan Honeycutt, 28, and a respected employee of Callahan, Inc., had been with the company for 6 years, earning recognition for his dedication and hard work. The news of his untimely demise has left colleagues and friends in shock and grief. Callahan, Inc. released a statement expressing condolences to Honeycutt's family and emphasizing the impact of his loss on the company.

Investigators are appealing to the public for any witnesses to come forward who may have seen the accident. The collision has prompted renewed discussions about AI-managed railways and the need for enhanced safety measures to prevent such tragedies.

The "accident" had happened just hours ago, yet Callahan, Inc. already had their statement polished and ready. No wonder Samantha had looked disheveled at breakfast—orchestrating a murder would do that to someone.

The brownstone lab, the brain scans that likely caused

Meredith's cancer, and now this. How far would the Callahans go to protect their secrets? My finger hovered over Officer Watts' number. But what could I tell her? That I suspected a powerful tech company had murdered their own employee?

James's "offer" tonight took on an even darker meaning. But maybe I had an ace up my sleeve—or rather, in my pocket. The marble Meredith had given me before she died felt warm against my palm. Last night's strange green glow hadn't been my imagination. I was hoping Alan had a clue. After all, he'd been at the conference where the tech had been discussed. Was this a storage device made from some kind of futuristic glass process? And would he have known how to access the data stored on it?

It could explain everything—why James had searched my hotel room, why they'd tried to scan my brain, why they'd ransacked my ranch.

I needed someone who could unlock its secrets. Someone who wasn't afraid of the Callahans. Someone who understood what was really at stake.

The pod door clicked open. I stepped out into FusionHub's chaos—a riot of screens and sounds, gamers lost in their virtual worlds. But through the digital mayhem, a familiar figure stopped me cold.

Aria.

She stood perfectly still amid the frenetic crowd, her presence as impossible as it was magnetic. Those eyes—Meredith's eyes—locked onto mine with an urgency that made my chest tight.

"Hello, Elijah." Her voice cut through the noise. "I have something to tell you."

**_Continued in Rebellion Protocol, Book 2 in the
Automated series._**

ABOUT THE AUTHOR

K. J. Gillenwater worked as a Russian linguist in the U.S. Navy, spending time at the National Security Agency doing secret things. After six years of service, she ended up as a technical writer in the software industry. She has lived all over the U.S. and currently resides in Wyoming with her family, writing government proposals and crafting captivating fiction on her days off. She likes her dogs, sunrises, and car radio karaoke.

Visit K.J.'s website for more information about her writing, her books, and what's coming next. www.kjgillenwater.com.

If you enjoyed this book, K. J. Gillenwater is the author of multiple books, which are available in print and in eBook format.

Full-length Books:

- The Automated Series: System Override, Rebellion Protocol
- The Genesis Machine Trilogy: Inception, Decryption, and Revelation
- The Aurora Series: Aurora's Gold and Aurora's Winter
- Revenge Honeymoon
- Illegal
- The Ninth Curse
- The Little Black Box

- Acapulco Nights
- Blood Moon

Short Stories & Short Story Collections:

- Skyfall
- Nemesis
- The Man in 14C
- Charlie and the Zombie Factory

Audiobooks (Audible):

- The Genesis Machine Trilogy: Inception, Decryption, and Revelation